PROMS

The BBC presents the 112th season
of Henry Wood Promenade Concerts

BBC
PROMS

WELCOME

to the BBC Proms 2006

Welcome to another summer of inspiring
music-making by the world's leading musicians,
as the BBC Proms 2006 present more concerts than
ever in a bigger, bolder festival of great music for all.

Two Giants of Music

This year we focus on two giants of the classical repertory: Wolfgang Amadeus Mozart (250 this year), *right*, and Dmitry Shostakovich (100 this year), *below*. The reputations of both composers are surrounded by controversy and myth; yet, however great the arguments over their lives, their music has never had more success than in the 21st century. Mozart's emotional ambiguity and Shostakovich's powerful statements both speak profoundly to our time.

Alongside a wealth of both composers' instrumental music, from Mozart's first symphony to Shostakovich's last, Glyndebourne brings Mozart's wonderfully subtle comedy *Così fan tutte*, Valery Gergiev and the Mariinsky Theatre bring Shostakovich's searingly tragic *Lady Macbeth of the Mtsensk District*, and Sir Charles Mackerras conducts a new completion of Mozart's unfinished C minor Mass. Our four Proms Films include Ingmar Bergman's enchanting version of Mozart's *The Magic Flute* and Kozintsev's powerful Russian *Hamlet*, with Shostakovich's original score.

Other Anniversaries of 2006

The Proms reach further in marking this year's other anniversaries, celebrating the masterpieces of Robert Schumann (who died 150 years ago), the *Requiem* of Michael Haydn (who died 200 years ago) and the court music of Marin Marais (born 350 years ago), as well as the work of leading international composers Henri Dutilleux (90), Hans Werner Henze and György Kurtág (both 80), Steve Reich (70) and Colin Matthews (60). Morton Feldman's music arrives at the Proms for the first time on his 80th anniversary.

The Best of the New

From the earliest days the Proms have had a mission to present the best of the world's new music; this year we bring to this country works by such leading composers of our time as HK Gruber, Magnus Lindberg and Wolfgang Rihm, and introduce outstanding new voices such as Dai Fujikura, Osvaldo Golijov and Toshio Hosokawa. We feature adventurous new British music and BBC commissions by Julian Anderson, George Benjamin, James Dillon, Jonathan Harvey, Mark-Anthony Turnage, Ian Wilson, and younger talent such as Benjamin Wallfisch.

The BBC Orchestras: A Time of Change

On the first night of the season, Jiří Bělohlávek (*above*) makes his debut as the new Chief Conductor of the BBC Symphony Orchestra; David Robertson conducts his first Proms as the BBC SO's new Principal Guest Conductor; associate artist John Adams conducts a programme of his own works; and Mark Elder returns to host the Last Night.

While Richard Hickox concludes an outstanding period at the helm of the BBC National Orchestra of Wales and Barry Wordsworth bows out as Principal Conductor of the BBC Concert Orchestra, Gianandrea Noseda and Ilan Volkov continue to thrill audiences with the BBC Philharmonic and the BBC Scottish Symphony Orchestra respectively.

Major Artists from Around the World

We welcome back conductors Christoph Eschenbach (carrying forward our four-year Proms *Ring* cycle), Bernard Haitink, Kurt Masur, Sir Simon Rattle (*below*), Esa-Pekka Salonen and many other leading names. Visiting orchestras – from Bamberg under Jonathan Nott and Budapest under Iván Fischer, to Pittsburgh under Sir Andrew Davis and Minnesota under Osmo Vänskä – plus Proms debuts from Stéphane Denève with the Royal Scottish National Orchestra, Philippe Jordan with the Gustav Mahler Youth Orchestra and a host of other major artists, together with a late-night celebration of Islamic music and culture, all add up to make the 2006 BBC Proms a truly international festival of outstanding talent.

A Tradition of Innovation

The Proms have always looked to the future, developing new formats and new audiences. This year we launch a special new series of Proms Saturday Matinees, showcasing leading chamber orchestras at Cadogan Hall; we highlight the human voice in a two-part choral day for everyone, with Orlando Gough and The Shout providing creative leadership; Charles Hazlewood (below, right) presents and conducts an innovative family concert with the BBC Concert Orchestra; and the Blue Peter Proms continue to raise the roof.

We are also delighted that Her Majesty The Queen will once again visit the Proms to hear a brand-new work for massed children's voices on which Sir Peter Maxwell Davies, the Master of the Queen's Music, and Andrew Motion, the Poet Laureate, have collaborated in honour of her 80th birthday.

The BBC: Bringing the Proms to You

As part of the BBC, the Proms also lead the way in bringing all this music to the widest possible audience – with every concert broadcast live on BBC Radio 3, many concerts also shown on BBC TV – including this year the whole of the last three weeks on BBC FOUR – and ever-wider interactive coverage on the internet.

So, wherever you are, enjoy the very best of classical music at the 2006 BBC Proms.

Nicholas Kenyon

Nicholas Kenyon
Director, BBC Proms

CONTENTS AT A GLANCE

THE PROMS
1895–2006

The Proms were founded to bring the best of classical music to a wide audience in an informal setting. From the very outset, part of the audience has always stood in the 'promenade'. Prom places originally cost just a shilling (5p); today, standing places at the Royal Albert Hall cost only £5, and over 1,000 tickets go on sale for every concert from an hour beforehand. Programmes have always mixed the great classics with what Henry Wood, the first conductor of the Proms, called his 'novelties' – in other words, rare works and premieres.

1895 The 26-year-old Henry Wood is chosen to launch the Promenade Concerts at the newly opened Queen's Hall, Langham Place; Wood conducts the Proms throughout their first 50 years. 1905 Wood composes his celebrated *Fantasia on British Sea-Songs* for a special Trafalgar Day concert. 1927 The BBC takes over the running of the Proms.

1930 The new BBC Symphony Orchestra becomes the orchestra of the Proms; the BBC's own orchestras still provide the backbone of the season. 1935 First pieces by Shostakovich heard at the Proms: the London concert premieres of Symphony No. 1 and 'Katharina's Song' from *Lady Macbeth of the Mtsensk District*.

1939 Proms season abandoned after only three weeks following the declaration of war and the evacuation of the BBC from London. 1940 Proms season (under the aegis of the Royal Philharmonic Society and with the LSO replacing the BBC SO) abandoned after only four weeks because of the Blitz. 1941 The Proms move to the Royal Albert Hall after the Queen's Hall is gutted in an air raid on 10 May.

1942 The BBC resumes responsibility for the Proms. The BBC SO shares the season for the first time with another orchestra: the London Philharmonic. First Proms performance of Parry's *Jerusalem* (incorporated into the Last Night in 1953). 1944 Wood dies shortly after celebrating his Proms jubilee.

1947 First televised Last Night. 1950 Malcolm Sargent becomes Chief Conductor of the BBCSO. 1953 First out-of-London orchestra at the Proms: the Hallé, from Manchester, under John Barbirolli. Wood's *Sea-Songs* are dropped from the Last Night schedule (in favour of Sargent's arrangement of *Rule, Britannia!*) but reinstated – as an encore – by public demand.

1955 First Proms appearance by the National Youth Orchestra. 1959 William Glock becomes the BBC's Controller of Music. 1960 William Alwyn's *Derby Day* launches a new BBC policy of regular Proms commissions for British composers. 1961 First complete opera heard at the Proms: Mozart's *Don Giovanni*, given by Glyndebourne Festival Opera.

1966 First foreign orchestra at the Proms: the Moscow Radio Orchestra, under Gennady Rozhdestvensky. 1967 Malcolm Sargent makes his final Proms appearance, speaking on the Last Night. 1968 First Friday-night First Night: memorial concert for Malcolm Sargent. 1970 First Late Night Prom: cult pop group The Soft Machine. 1971 First 'world music' Prom: sitar-player Imrat Khan. 1973 Robert Ponsonby succeeds William Glock.

1974 First Pre-Prom Talks. 1986 John Drummond becomes BBC Controller of Music. 1994 The Proms celebrate their 100th season with a retrospective of past premieres. 1995 The Proms celebrate their centenary year with a season of new commissions. 1996 Nicholas Kenyon becomes Director of the Proms. First Proms Chamber Music series; first Prom in the Park.

1997 First Proms solo recital: pianist Evgeny Kissin. 1998 First Blue Peter Family Prom. 2002 The Proms go digital with a fortnight of broadcasts on the new BBC FOUR and the start of on-demand listening online. 2003 Proms in the Park expands to embrace all four nations of the UK. The Proms go fully interactive on digital satellite and Freeview television.

2005 First Proms Films series at the Royal Geographical Society. Proms Chamber Music moves to Cadogan Hall. Henry Wood's *Fantasia on British Sea-Songs* celebrates its centenary in a new revised version (with restored bugle calls). 2006 First Proms Saturday Matinees at Cadogan Hall.

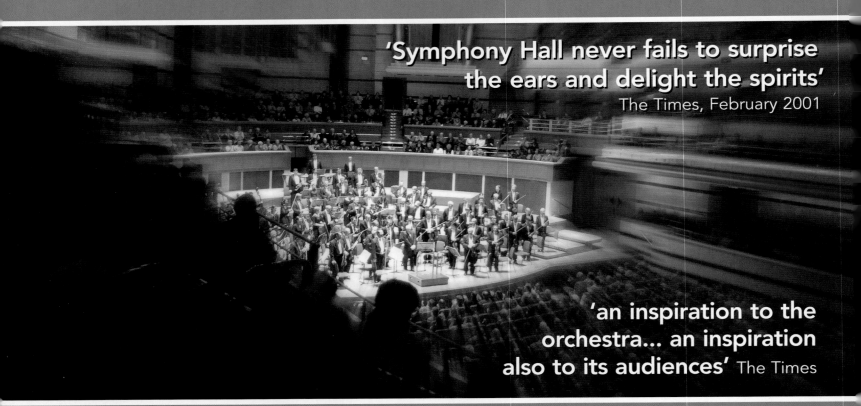

symphony hall
birmingham

'Symphony Hall never fails to surprise the ears and delight the spirits'
The Times, February 2001

'an inspiration to the orchestra... an inspiration also to its audiences' The Times

'The best concert hall in the country'
Daily Telegraph

box office 0121 780 3333
online box office www.symphonyhall.co.uk/boxoffice
www.symphonyhall.co.uk admin tel: +44 (0)121 200 2000
fax: +44 (0)121 212 1982 email: symphonyhall@necgroup.co.uk

B&W Bowers & Wilkins

The new B&W 800 Series
Diamond Tweeter Technology

Diamond
At Work

> *R E L E A S E D*

The mark of a truly great tweeter – one that can release all the vivid detail in your music – is what's called 'perfect piston behaviour'. As long as the tweeter dome is vibrating rigidly, like a piston, its delivery will be accurate. The higher the frequency, though, the harder that becomes. The materials most resistant to 'break-up' combine lightness and stiffness. And there's one that does that better than anything else on earth.

The new B&W 800 Series feature tweeter domes of pure, ultra-hard diamond. It may seem extravagant, but nothing gets closer to the behaviour of a hypothetical 'perfect tweeter' – one with infinite stiffness. Our diamond dome carries on vibrating like a piston well beyond the range of human hearing, and delivers audible sound with unheard-of clarity.

www.bw800.com
Visit our website and order your free DVD
Call +44 (0)1903 221 500

*Only 800 Series models with this symbol use
B&W diamond tweeter technology*

English National Opera's
Summer Season 2006

ENO

Madam Butterfly

Anthony Minghella's stunning, award-nominated production of **Puccini**'s masterpiece returns to ENO after its initial sell-out run last autumn. Leading soprano **Janice Watson** makes her debut in the title role. **David Parry** conducts.

'**The hottest opera ticket in London**' The Sunday Times

APR 29 · MAY 5 · 10 · 12 · 16 · 25 · 27 · 31
8 performances only.

The Makropulos Case

A poignant new production of **Janáček**'s enigmatic opera, conducted by **Sir Charles Mackerras** and directed by **Christopher Alden**. The cast is led by **Cheryl Barker** in her role debut and **Robert Brubaker**.

MAY 18 · 20 · 24 · 26 · 30 · JUNE 2 · 7 · 9
8 performances only. NEW PRODUCTION

Ariodante

Handel's inspired romantic masterpiece returns to the London Coliseum. **Alice Coote** takes the title role whilst **Patricia Bardon**, **Rebecca Evans** and **Peter Rose** lend their talent to the exceptional ensemble. Originally directed by **David Alden**.

'**One of ENO's defining operatic productions...
simply not to be missed.**' The Guardian

JUNE 1 · 3 · 8 · 10 · 13 · 16 · 22 · 24
8 performances only.

Nixon in China

ENO revives **Peter Sellars**'s powerful production of **John Adams**'s modern classic. **James Maddalena** and **Janis Kelly** reprise their original roles and **Paul Daniel** conducts. With choreography by **Mark Morris**.

'**On no account should it be missed**' The Daily Telegraph

JUNE 14 · 17 · 23 · 29 · JULY 6
5 performances only.

King Arthur

Mark Morris's joyous interpretation of **Purcell**'s rarely performed opera. Designer **Adrianne Lobel**, conductor **Jane Glover** and the **Mark Morris Dance Group** collaborate with an impressive line-up of award-winning soloists in this much anticipated world premiere.

JUNE 26 · 27 · 28 · 30 · JULY 1 · 3 · 4 · 5 · 7 · 8
10 performances only. NEW PRODUCTION

Tickets £10 – £84

ENO live at the London Coliseum
**Buy online www.eno.org
or call 0870 145 0200**
London Coliseum, St Martin's Lane, London WC2N 4ES

FABIO LUISI

GENERAL MUSIC DIRECTOR FROM 07/08

SOUND & SPLENDOUR   STAATSKAPELLE
SINCE 1548   DRESDEN

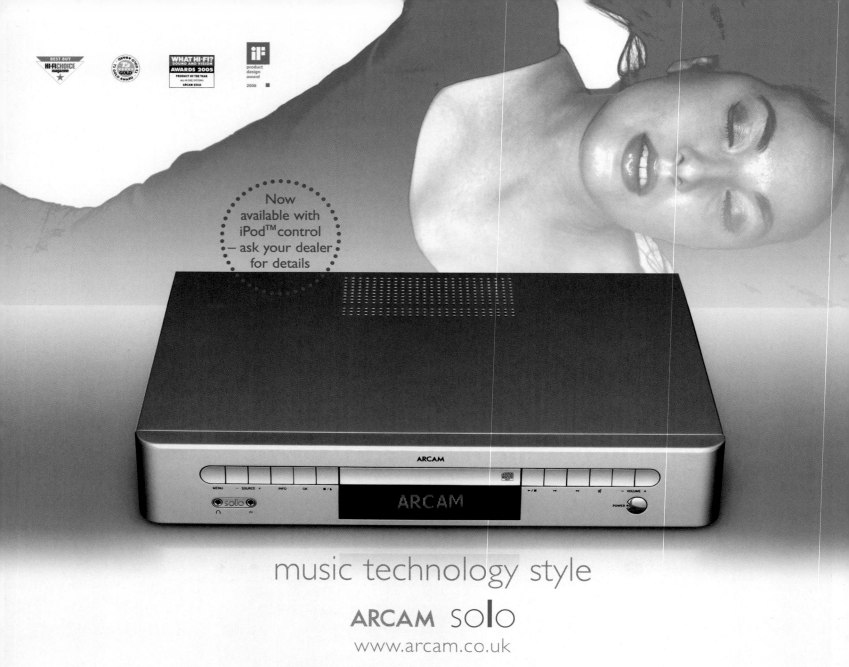

Now available with iPod™ control – ask your dealer for details

music technology style

ARCAM solo
www.arcam.co.uk

integrated high fidelity – pure and simple

13 August - 3 September
FESTIVAL 2006

From the first notes of Strauss's **Elektra** at the **Opening Concert** on **Sunday 13 August** through the world premiere of Stuart MacRae's opera **The Assassin Tree**, **Claudio Abbado** conducting **Die Zauberflöte**, Opéra National de Lyon performing Tchaikovsky's **Mazeppa**, recitals from **Richard Goode, Soile Isokoski, Jonas Kaufmann, Christian Zacharias, Simon Keenlyside** and **Pieter Wispelwey** and a host of visiting orchestras, to a concert performance of **Die Meistersinger von Nürnberg** on **Saturday 2 September** the **Edinburgh International Festival** is an intense and powerful three weeks of world class music. And then there's the programme of international drama and fantastic classical and contemporary dance …

EDINBURGH
INTERNATIONAL
FESTIVAL

Browse the programme and book for all Edinburgh International Festival performances online
www.eif.co.uk or call **0131 473 2000** for a free brochure

The many faces of
MOZART

Richard Wigmore surveys changing attitudes to the composer's music in the two and a half centuries since his birth

'Too many notes, my dear Mozart, and too beautiful for our ears.' Emperor Joseph II's celebrated reaction to Mozart's first Viennese opera, *Die Entführung aus dem Serail* ('The Abduction from the Seraglio'), may be apocryphal. But the alleged royal critique does highlight a recurrent problem posed by Mozart's music. The richness, intricacy and emotional ambivalence that so delight us today were often ▶

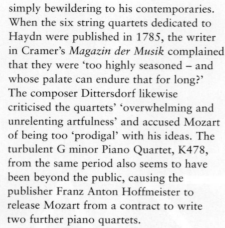

simply bewildering to his contemporaries. When the six string quartets dedicated to Haydn were published in 1785, the writer in Cramer's *Magazin der Musik* complained that they were 'too highly seasoned – and whose palate can endure that for long?' The composer Dittersdorf likewise criticised the quartets' 'overwhelming and unrelenting artfulness' and accused Mozart of being too 'prodigal' with his ideas. The turbulent G minor Piano Quartet, K478, from the same period also seems to have been beyond the public, causing the publisher Franz Anton Hoffmeister to release Mozart from a contract to write two further piano quartets.

It would be absurd, of course, to portray Mozart as an isolated, Romantic figure out of step with his age. Like Haydn, he was often adept at balancing the demands of *Kenner* – 'connoisseurs' – and less sophisticated listeners. He famously remarked to his father that his first Viennese piano concertos (Nos. 11–13, K413–15), composed in the winter of 1782–3, were 'a happy medium between what is too easy and too difficult' – a verdict that can be extended to the six glorious concertos of 1784, written at a time when Mozart, confounding his father's dire warnings, was riding the crest of a wave as a composer-virtuoso.

Even in such a complex and challenging work as the C minor Concerto (No. 24, K491) of 1786, the *faux-naïf* theme of the slow movement and the sensuous serenading episodes for woodwind are instantly beguiling. And though they far transcend their humble *Singspiel* origins, both *Die Entführung* (which, despite the Emperor, became Mozart's greatest success in his lifetime) and his final triumph, *Die Zauberflöte* ('The Magic Flute'), brilliantly exploited Viennese popular taste, most obviously in Papageno's antics and such comic numbers as the drinking duet for Pedrillo and Osmin in *Die Entführung*.

The Viennese were less euphoric, though, about the three great Da Ponte comedies. Despite the obligatory intrigues and hostile claques, *Figaro* was a fair success on its premiere in Vienna in 1786, but far from the runaway hit it soon became in Prague. When it came to comic opera, the Viennese – and not only the Viennese – preferred the breezy, undemanding fare of composers such as Paisiello and Martín y Soler. Four years later *Così fan tutte* was admired for the beauty of its music but increasingly attacked for its supposedly frivolous and immoral libretto. But it was *Don Giovanni* that in Mozart's lifetime proved the most controversial of the operas outside Prague, where it was first

'I could never compose operas like *Don Juan* and *Figaro* – they are too frivolous … I could never have got myself into a mood for such licentious texts'

Ludwig van Beethoven

LE NOZZE
DI FIGARO,
O SIA
LA FOLLE GIORNATA.
COMEDIA PER MUSICA
TRATTA DAL FRANCESE
IN QUATTRO ATTI.

DA RAPPRESENTARSI
Nei Teatri di Praga
l'Anno 1786.

Preso Giuseppe Emanuele Diesbach.

PREVIOUS PAGE
'A pop star in a powdered wig': woodcut portrait of Mozart after a sculpture by Wilhelm Hagen *(left)* and Tom Hulce as a 'manic, foul-mouthed' Mozart in Milos Forman's 1984 film of Peter Shaffer's *Amadeus*

ABOVE
Title-page from a libretto published for the Prague premiere of *The Marriage of Figaro*: as Mozart wrote to a friend in January 1787, 'Here they talk of nothing but *Figaro*; nothing is played, sung or whistled but *Figaro*; no opera is drawing like *Figaro*; nothing, nothing but *Figaro* …'

LEFT
Papageno the birdcatcher, adding a populist touch to Mozart's *The Magic Flute*: costume design for an 1816 Berlin production

performed in 1787 and where, as the composer observed, he was 'understood' more than anywhere else. On its Viennese premiere a year later, Joseph II (more reliably documented this time) declared that 'Mozart's music is certainly too difficult to be sung'. (In his memoirs, Da Ponte quotes the Emperor as saying, 'The opera is divine, perhaps even finer than *Figaro*, but it is not food for the Viennese' – to which Mozart crisply retorted, 'Let us give them time to chew it!') Though he was to be proved spectacularly wrong, one German critic spoke for many when he wrote: 'The beauty, greatness and nobility of the music for *Don Juan* will never appeal anywhere to more than a handful of the elect. It is not music to everyone's taste, merely tickling the ear and letting the heart starve.'

A decade after Mozart's death, even a critic as sympathetic to the composer as Johann Friedrich Rochlitz could write in the influential *Allgemeine musikalische Zeitung* that 'many of his fully textured compositions are congested, his modulations not infrequently bizarre, his transitions rough ... rarely is he delicate without emitting painful, tension-laden sighs' – a judgement we might expect to be applied to Beethoven rather than Mozart. By then, though, Mozart's greatness was acknowledged throughout Europe, and the myth-makers were getting to work.

What was simply 'bizarre' to Rochlitz was charged with mysterious, supernatural force for that weaver of fantastic tales, E. T. A. Hoffmann. Hoffmann saw in Mozart's instrumental music 'an intimation of infinity', and was the first to stress the

'Does it not seem as if Mozart's works become fresher and fresher the oftener we hear them?'

Robert Schumann

'demonic' element in *Don Giovanni*, the Mozart work that haunted the 19th century more than any other. *Don Giovanni* provided the springboard for works of fiction and philosophy, beginning with Hoffmann's own short story *Don Juan* and continuing with Eduard Mörike's widely read novella *Mozart auf der Reise nach Prag* ('Mozart's Journey to Prague'), where the composer is inspired by voices from another world, and the Danish philosopher Kierkegaard's *Either/Or*, where the Don becomes an abstract embodiment of desire, feverishly seeking a Goethean ideal of womanhood.

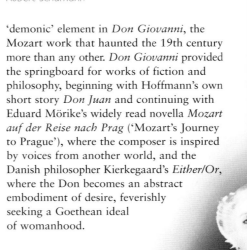

This German Romantic view of a Dionysian, demonically inspired Mozart, at his most characteristic in works like *Don Giovanni*, the *Requiem* and the two minor-key piano concertos (No. 20, K466, and No. 24, K491) – significantly, his only two concertos to enter the regular 19th-century repertoire – was the virtual antithesis of another, more widely held notion: that of Mozart the eternal child, an image spawned by the reminiscences of his sister Nannerl and given a late-20th-century gloss in the play and film *Amadeus*. As the 19th century progressed, Mozart's music was increasingly identified with innocence and purity. Far from being a 'difficult' composer, he became the paragon of Classical grace and order. Where Mozart's late minor-key works had once seemed bizarre and 'extreme', Robert Schumann revealingly described the G minor Symphony (No. 40) as a work of 'Grecian lightness and grace'.

For many musicians, including Tchaikovsky, Mozart was revered as the touchstone of serene beauty, idealised as the emblem of a lost Eden. Yet for the wider 19th-century public he lagged far behind Beethoven in popularity. Only a tiny percentage of his works – notably *Figaro*, *Don Giovanni*, *Die Zauberflöte*, the unfinished *Requiem*, the last three symphonies and the two minor-key piano concertos – were regularly performed. *Idomeneo*, eloquently described by David Cairns in his new book on the operas as 'a secular Passion, with a power to chasten and uplift a distracted age', was dismissed as a chilly museum piece. *Così fan tutte*, whose unresolved ambiguities and unique mix of brittle cynicism, parody and dreamlike radiance make it Mozart's most disquieting and 'relevant' opera for many listeners today, was condemned as laughably trivial and (not least by Beethoven and Wagner) an insult to the dignity of women.

While Nannerl's memories of the early Salzburg years gave rise to the legend of the perpetual child, and long coloured perceptions of his music, it was Mozart's wife Constanze who, with evident self-interest, did more than anyone to create the sentimental picture of the pure-hearted genius, under-appreciated and under-rewarded, his only fault (and on this she and Nannerl were agreed) his inability to handle money. Mozart certainly left his family ill-provided-for at his death, partly because of Constanze's costly spa cures. Though he tended to spend as fast as he earned (and on occasion faster), modern research has shown that for most of the Viennese years he made a handsome living from teaching, commissions and the performance and publication of his works, especially concertos and chamber music. Despite his debts at the time of his death, 1791 – in contrast to the relatively lean period of 1788–90 – had been one of his most profitable years. Future prospects, not least a lucrative offer to compose and supervise operas in London, looked even better.

The Romantic age, though, needed heroes, rebels and tragic victims, preferably all rolled into one. So we got Mozart the subversive, setting Beaumarchais's *Figaro* as a defiant challenge to the social and political status quo. There was Mozart the solitary visionary, composing his last three symphonies (Nos. 39–41) in his ivory tower, without prospect of performance. But Mozart, like Beethoven, never wrote for posterity. The symphonies were almost certainly intended for a series of subscription concerts in the autumn of 1788; and whether or not these took place, Mozart would have

BELOW & LEFT
Lorenzo da Ponte, librettist of Mozart's three great Viennese comedies, and Eduard Engerth's *Figaro* fresco at the Vienna State Opera

RIGHT
Salzburg, the Austrian city where Mozart was born and bred, with *(inset, from top)* Mozart himself at the ages of 7 (anon.), 14 (Louis Gabriel Blanchet) and 24, with his sister and father and a portrait of his dead mother on the wall (Johann Nepomuk della Croce)

'I tell you before God and as an honest man that your son is the greatest composer known to me; he has taste and in addition the most complete knowledge of composition'

Joseph Haydn, to Mozart's father Leopold, 1785

LEFT
Cloaked in mystery:
the anonymous masked
messenger from Milos
Forman's film *Amadeus* and
the final bars from Mozart's
uncompleted autograph

BELOW
Mozart's supposed murderer,
the imperial court composer
Antonio Salieri (anonymous
portrait)

Many of the Mozart myths that took root in the 19th century lingered on well into the 20th. Even Alfred Einstein's thoughtful and affectionate biography of 1944 – still one of the most influential books in the vast Mozart literature – perpetuates the view that 'Mozart was a child, and always remained one' – albeit a child given to financial extravagance and sensual excess. Only in the past half-century, with the work of writers like H. C. Robbins Landon, Wolfgang Hildesheimer, Volkmar Braunbehrens and Maynard Solomon, have the sentimentalising, romanticising images been subject to serious, scholarly scrutiny. True, *Amadeus* – the 1984 film, far more than the play on which it was based – gave the myth of the eternal child a contemporary twist, making the composer a manic, foul-mouthed brat-rebel, a pop star in a powdered wig. In Peter Shaffer's clever conceit, Mozart is an unworthy conduit for divine inspiration: in the words of his antagonist Salieri, 'a giggling child who can put on paper, without actually setting down his billiard cue, casual notes which can turn my most considered ones into lifeless scratches'. Yet as far as we can ever know him, Mozart was a complex, restless man, in whom worldliness coexisted with idealism, irresponsibility with a shrewd business acumen (he was a brilliant impresario in the early Viennese years), a lifelong penchant for the bawdy and the zany (which only enhanced his humanity for the late 20th century) with an increasing tendency to melancholy introspection: a man of flesh and blood, and a rigorously self-critical artist who, *pace* Shaffer and

'Didn't I tell you that I was composing the *Requiem* for myself?'

Mozart on his deathbed, as quoted in the biography by Georg Nikolaus Nissen, Constanze's second husband

had several opportunities to perform them in the remaining three years of his life. The unfinished *Requiem*, commissioned in unusual (though certainly not lurid) circumstances – an anonymous count with ideas above his artistic station simply wanted to pass the work off as his own – proved a gift to the febrile Romantic imagination: the count's steward 'cloaked in grey' became an emissary from another world, while Mozart in his delirium imagined he was writing the *Requiem* for himself. Then there was the scandal of the pauper's grave, the ultimate proof of Viennese neglect and incomprehension. The less sensational truth was that Mozart, like most middle-class Viennese, was buried in a communal grave in St Marx's cemetery, in keeping with the custom for modest, economical burials initiated by Joseph II.

ABOVE
Mozart, the last likeness: unfinished portrait by his brother-in-law Joseph Lange

RIGHT
Mozart, the last word in bad taste? A Salzburg shop window full of edible anniversary memorabilia

the Romantic myth-makers before him, did not compose somnambulistically but would often make extensive sketches before a theme or passage emerged to his satisfaction.

Two and a half centuries after his birth 'the miracle that God let be born in Salzburg', to quote his father, is enthroned as the most popular of all Classical composers: the most played, the most psychoanalysed, the most deconstructed (not least by opera producers), the most commercially exploited (as the retailers of Salzburg and Prague will be happy to confirm). His genius is rightly hailed as universal, protean. The grace and surface prettiness of his music – which the 19th century tended to equate with shallowness – appeals to the most casual listener. Yet beyond this, his mercurial, ambivalent, ultimately elusive vision – at once smiling and unsettling, life-affirming and shadowed with intimations of mortality – speaks with a unique poignancy and power to our fractured, disturbed times. As Maynard Solomon has memorably written, 'Mozart is one of those rare creative beings who come to disturb the sleep of the world. He was put on earth, it seems, not merely to provide an anodyne to our sorrow and an antidote to loss, but to trouble our rest, to remind us … that things are not what they seem to be, that masquerade and reality may well be interchangeable, that love is frail, life transient, faith unstable.'

MOZART AT THE PROMS
For a full list of Mozart's music being performed at this year's Proms, see the Index of Works, pages 156–9
• See also Proms Films, page 120

'How seemly, then, to celebrate the birth
Of one who did no harm to our poor earth,
Created masterpieces by the dozen,
Indulged in toilet-humour with his cousin,
And had a pauper's funeral in the rain,
The like of whom we shall not see again …'
W. H. Auden, 'Metalogue to The Magic Flute', 1956

Remembrance Travel

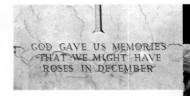

RBL Village, AYLESFORD, ME20 7NX
Tel: 01622 716729 or 716182 Fax: 01622 715768
Email: remembrancetravel@britishlegion.org.uk
Website: www.remembrancetravel.com

✔ Do you want to visit the grave or memorial of a relative or friend overseas?

✔ Are you a War Widow / Widower whose spouse died between 1914-1967 and who has not travelled back to see the grave of your husband / wife before at MOD expense?

✔ Do you have an interest in WWI and WWII battlefields?

WE CAN HELP

✤ For the last 21 years Remembrance Travel has been organising pilgrimages to War Cemeteries and tours to Battlefields Worldwide and has acted as the MOD official agents

✤ If you are eligible, the Government has a grant that will pay 100% of a Widow or Widower's costs to visit the grave, either on one of our pilgrimages or under individual arrangements – **call for more details**

✤ We have pilgrimages and battlefield tours that cover

✤ Belgium to Burma ✤
✤ France to the Falklands ✤
✤ Italy to India ✤
✤ Holland to Hong Kong ✤

✔ Anyone can join one of our tours – you do not have to be a Royal British Legion member

✔ Anyone can join one of our tours – you do not have to be visiting a specific grave

Whatever your interest, please contact Remembrance Travel for a full colour brochure detailing all tours this year or take a look at our website which has all of the details.

BBC Symphony Orchestra

Join the BBC Symphony Orchestra and our new

Chief Conductor
Jiří Bělohlávek

for a season of exciting and distinctive concerts.

Highlights of the 2006/07 season include:
- Beethoven's Symphony No. 3 'Eroica'
- A weekend celebrating the music of Sofia Gubaidulina
- Janáček's *The Excursions of Mr Brouček*
- World premieres of works by Simon Bainbridge, Jonathan Dove, Michael Nyman and John Tavener

Flagship Orchestra of the BBC Proms
Associate Orchestra of the Barbican

All concerts in the BBC Symphony Orchestra's 2006/07 Barbican season are on sale now.

Visit **bbc.co.uk/symphonyorchestra** for full details and to book your tickets.
Call the Barbican Box Office from May for a free season brochure.

barbican

Box Office
020 7638 8891 (bkg fee)
www.barbican.org.uk
Reduced booking fee online

BBC RADIO 3
90-93 FM

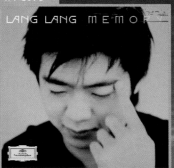

The Sage Gateshead

The Sage Gateshead is an international home for music and musical discovery

The Sage Gateshead occupies one of the most dramatic urban sites in Europe, on the River Tyne. It houses performance spaces of acoustic excellence with state-of-the art facilities, quality catering, licensed bars and excellent road, rail and air links.

For further details contact The Sage Gateshead's Performance Programme Co-ordinator on +44 (0) 191 443 4666 or e-mail HallBookings@thesagegateshead.org

Hall One   Hall Two

Northern Sinfonia

Music Director, Thomas Zehetmair

Northern Sinfonia, orchestra of The Sage Gateshead.

"45 minutes of utterly committed, passionately driven, spine tinglingly exhilarating music-making. Beautiful hardly begins to describe it. A scintillating event." *The Times*

"This is the sort of stimulating brew that is fast becoming one of the hallmarks of the Sinfonia's programming policy under its new music director, Thomas Zehetmair." *The Daily Telegraph*

For further details contact Simon Clugston, Performance Programme Director on +44 (0) 191 443 4666 or e-mail simon.clugston@thesagegateshead.org

with funding from the European Regional Development Fund

NewcastleGateshead
world-class culture

north east
england

ARTS COUNCIL
ENGLAND

one
NorthEast

Gateshead
Council

Photography: Alex Telfer, Richard Bryant

EDUCATING
THE MUSICIANS OF TOMORROW

Do you know a child with a special talent in music?

The UK's five specialist
music schools exist to
provide a unique
world-class education.

Come and visit us

St Mary's Music School,
Coates Hall, 25 Grosvenor Crescent,
Edinburgh EH12 5EL
Tel. 0131 538 7766
www.st-marys-music-school.co.uk

The Purcell School,
Aldenham Road,
Bushey, Herts WD23 2TS
Tel. 01923 331100
www.purcell-school.org

Yehudi Menuhin School,
Cobham Road, Stoke d'Abernon,
Cobham, Surrey KT11 3QQ
Tel. 01932 864739
www.yehudimenuhinschool.co.uk

Chetham's School of Music,
Long Millgate,
Manchester M3 1SB
Tel. 0161 834 9644
www.chethams.com

Wells Cathedral School,
Wells, Somerset
BA5 2ST
Tel: 01749 834250
www.wells-cathedral-school.com

Government funding is available for
UK residents providing up to 100% of fees.

Visit the DfES website: www.dfes.gov.uk/mds
for more information about the
music and dance scheme.

NAMDS

THE NATIONAL ASSOCIATION
OF MUSIC AND DANCE SCHOOLS

www.namds.org.uk

The secret life of
SHOS

TAKOVICH

Composer or hero? **Dennis Marks** tries to find the human face behind the public mask

'There are heroes and there are composers,' said Arnold Schoenberg of Dmitry Shostakovich in 1944. 'Heroes can be composers and vice versa; but you cannot require it.' In this centenary year it is worth asking the question: which Shostakovich are we celebrating – the composer or the hero? Sixty years ago, there was a straightforward answer. An iconic photograph on the cover of *Time* magazine showed the composer wearing a fireman's helmet on the roof ▶

Lebrecht Music & Arts (p28) RIA Novosti (p30 left)

LEFT
'An attempt to look into the future, into the post-war era': Shostakovich at work on his Eighth Symphony in Moscow in August 1943

of the Philharmonic Hall, glaring myopically through thick spectacles as the Leningrad night sky crackled under German bombardment. Here was the honoured Soviet artist Dmitry Dmitryevich, creator of the 'Leningrad' Symphony, embodying the heroic resistance of the Russian people to Nazi aggression. If we spool on three decades to 1974, the year before his death, we find a very different photograph, taken at the premiere of his last string quartet. His face is drawn, his lips are pursed. This is the portrait of a reluctant, compromised public figure, taking temporary refuge in the privacy of chamber music.

How do we reconcile these two icons? Perhaps we should consider a third, this time expressed in words. In 1979 Harper and Row published *Testimony: The Memoirs of Dmitry Shostakovich, as Related to and Edited by Solomon Volkov*. This controversial little volume presented a third iconic image – a bitter and sardonic victim of the state, who had spent his creative life delivering what the critic Richard Taruskin has ironically described as 'messages in bottles'. According to *Testimony*, Shostakovich's epic celebrations of Soviet achievement were nothing of the sort: they were coded indictments of totalitarian oppression and the composer was a different species of hero – a musical dissident, a Solzhenitsyn with a symphony orchestra.

These contradictory icons have two things in common – each of them has been discredited and none of them tells us anything about the music. Just as Volkov's transcribed 'memoirs' had swept away all the Soviet heroics, so within a year of its release a posse of academics had challenged

the authenticity of *Testimony* itself. The seven pages in the book's original typescript signed by the composer with the words 'read by Dmitry Shostakovich' were revealed to be verbatim transcripts of statements already published in his lifetime and clumsily inserted into Volkov's text. While Shostakovich the hero dissolved like the smile on the face of the Cheshire Cat, Shostakovich the composer receded still further from our view.

No-one is more culpable than film-makers when it comes to peppering the music with distracting biographical dust. From the late 1970s, directors (myself included) have queued up to present it as the soundtrack to a Cold War thriller. From Tony Palmer's accomplished drama based on *Testimony* and Peter Maniura's painstaking documentary *A Career* to Larry Weinstein's garish *War Symphonies* and my own series *All the Russias* (shown on BBC4 in 2003), we have all been tempted to swallow the Volkov line of 'Shostakovich the symphonic dissident' more or less undigested. This is doubly unfortunate. On the one hand, it encourages those critics who dismiss the music as hysterical pictorialism; on the other, it fails to do justice to the profound skill with which the composer translated film aesthetic into musical language. Indeed, there is an argument that Shostakovich was saved by film. It gave him both a personal idiom and a livelihood at a time when creative artists had never been more vulnerable.

Shostakovich was the first great 20th-century composer to find a home in the cinema and he was absorbed in film from the very beginning of his working life. In

1924, at the age of 18, during the harsh years that followed the Civil War, he augmented the meagre family income by improvising soundtracks on the piano at the Bright Reel and Splendid Palace cinemas in Leningrad. It was enervating work but it provided an opportunity to develop his musical language. It also brought him into intimate contact with the prevailing aesthetic values of the early Soviet Union. Lenin always regarded the cinema as 'for us the most important of all the arts'. He commissioned cinema trains to travel the length and breadth of Russia showing educational and propagandist documentaries. Stalin was an even more passionate cinema-lover. There are tales of the leader dragooning his commissars into his private cinema in the Kremlin, where they watched interminable screenings of popular movies until the early hours. *The Great Waltz* and *Tarzan* were particular favourites.

In the 1920s, when the doctrine of Socialist Realism actively encouraged experiment and artistic risk, Russian directors more or less invented the art of montage. The arrival of sound at the end of the decade provided further opportunities for creative adventure. In their *Statement on Sound*, Eisenstein and Pudovkin wrote: 'The first experiments in sound must aim at a sharp discord with the visual images.' This is exactly what we experience in Shostakovich's early film scores. In one of his few authentic statements on his craft, the 23-year-old composer described how he approached Kozintsev and Trauberg's forceful and ironic drama of the Paris Commune, *The New Babylon*: 'It is

'When a critic writes that in such-and-such a symphony Soviet civil servants are represented by the oboe and clarinet, and Red Army men by the brass section, it makes me want to scream!'

Dmitry Shostakovich

time to take cinema music in hand, to eliminate the bungling and the inartistic ...' His first scores carried the language of collage from the cinema into the concert hall and the opera house. The jagged outlines of the first three symphonies are the musical equivalent of the fractured continuity in Dziga Vertov's pioneering documentary *Man with a Movie Camera*. Musical montage was pushed to the limits in Shostakovich's early opera *The Nose* and the sardonic third act of his *Lady Macbeth of the Mtsensk District*, which intriguingly

31

'The power of good music to enthral the masses has been sacrificed on the altar of petty-bourgeois formalism … This is a game of clever ingenuity that may end very badly'

From 'Chaos Instead of Music', the notorious critique of 'Lady Macbeth', published in 'Pravda' on 28 January 1936

originated in an abandoned scheme for a musical feature film. And nothing could be more fragmented and discontinuous than the opening movement of the Fourth Symphony.

Needless to say, this did not last. By 1932 Socialist Realism was required to celebrate Soviet achievement not with bold experimentation but with accessible melodies and heroic choruses. Shostakovich was not immune to these pressures. Nevertheless, even after 1936, when *Lady Macbeth* was officially castigated in *Pravda* and the Fourth Symphony withdrawn in rehearsal, his music maintained much of its characteristic style and structure. The Fifth Symphony (apologetically dubbed 'a Soviet artist's creative reply to just criticism') may wear conventional clothes, but in their own fashion the Sixth, Eighth and Ninth all defy the monumental symmetry now required of Soviet art. This gives the lie to the stereotypes of loyal Soviet citizen, timorous hack and closet dissident. Not only did Shostakovich preserve a great deal of his artistic integrity, but for a decade after the *Pravda* débâcle the state continued to turn a blind eye and afforded him a high level of official protection and support. In 1946, despite the chilly reception accorded to his Eighth and Ninth Symphonies, he could still write to Stalin thanking him for arranging a stipend of 60,000 roubles and a five-room apartment. His score and theme song for the 1932 movie *The Counterplan* remained among Stalin's personal favourites, even when other distinguished Soviet artists were being robbed of their livelihoods, their freedom and sometimes their lives.

Without doubt, Shostakovich was scarred both as a composer and as a human being when, in 1948, Stalin's cultural commissar Andrey Zhdanov denounced Soviet music for its 'formalist cosmopolitan tendencies'. In the following five years Shostakovich wrote some of his least distinguished music, much of it for state occasions and a few eminently forgettable films. Yet the two major works premiered in the mid-1950s, shortly after Stalin's death, both reveal how his musical language remained essentially intact. The Tenth Symphony, completed while Stalin was still alive but kept under wraps, has long been acknowledged as a desolate depiction of loss. The composer Gerard McBurney has, however, recently revealed that enfolded in the thematic material are references to a secret love-affair. The social and personal

LEFT
The New Babylon: the 1929 Kozintsev and Trauberg silent film for which the 23-year-old Shostakovich composed a 90-minute score in just two weeks

BELOW
Lady Macbeth: the murder scene from the 1935 Bolshoy Theatre staging that so upset Stalin and prompted *Pravda*'s notorious attack on the composer under the headline 'Chaos Instead of Music' *(top right)*

RIGHT
Shostakovich, flanked by Leonid Brezhnev (left), the General Secretary of the Communist Party, and Alexey Kosygin, the Premier of the USSR, at the opening of the Fourth All-Union Congress of Composers in December 1968; and reading a copy of *Pravda* in May 1965

'A loyal son of the Communist Party, an outstanding public figure and statesman, the artist-citizen D. D. Shostakovich devoted his entire life to the development of Soviet music, to asserting the ideals of socialist humanism and internationalism, to the struggle for peace and friendship among nations'

From Shostakovich's obituary notice in 'Pravda', 12 August 1975

'Time has a way of demonstrating that the most stubborn are the most intelligent … We've forgotten the men who abused them, we remember only the victims of their slander … I shall therefore pursue my career by trying not to pursue one!'

Lines by Yevgeny Yevtushenko, set by Shostakovich in his 'Babi Yar' Symphony of 1962

The Eleventh, composed soon after the Khrushchev 'thaw', is even more ambivalent. While its subtitle 'The Year 1905' suggests a celebration of Russia's first failed revolution, some of the composer's colleagues begged to differ. Solomon Volkov, the critic Lev Lebedinsky and the poet Anna Akhmatova have variously implied that the score carried hidden messages about the Soviet invasion of Hungary and the continuing existence of the gulags. Yet the 19th-century prison songs quoted throughout the work suggest that, if there is a message, it is less specific and more desperate – that human oppression is cyclical and its consequences are always with us.

In the 1960s the ambivalence continued. The Socialist Realist Twelfth Symphony and the cantata *The Execution of Stepan Razin* sat side by side with the fierce protest of the Yevtushenko settings in the Thirteenth Symphony, 'Babi Yar'. When, in his final slow retreat into the private world of chamber music, he revisited the experiments of his youth and toyed with his own version of serialism, Shostakovich's creative language remained essentially the same. The fractured collage of the last two symphonies harks back to the first three. The becalmed adagios in the final string quartets are the logical extension of the slow movements of the works written in the 1940s.

If there are messages in these last works, they are sent by Shostakovich to himself. If there are codes, they are personal ones. Some of them relate to his approaching death, some to his foreshortened youth and others are almost

are interwoven. In the finale the personal gains the upper hand: the composer's musical signature – the notes D, E flat, C and B, which in German notation spell out his initials DSCH – gradually shove all the other thematic material into the margins, asserting that whatever else happens, inside or outside, his identity is indestructible.

impossible to penetrate. Above all, they contain testimony that is impossible to discredit – to the deep friendships with other musicians like Rostropovich and Britten, which have left us such legacies as the two cello concertos, the Fourteenth Symphony and the *Michelangelo Suite*. So, if we still seek a map through his private labyrinth, we are most likely to find it in his letters to his friend and amanuensis Isaak Glikman or in Elizabeth Wilson's detailed and deeply touching collection of interviews with contemporaries and colleagues (soon to be reissued in an enlarged edition). On a journey through the composer's life, these books are more rewarding companions than questionable memoirs or the speculations of commentators and film-makers. Best of all, in this centenary year, are the many opportunities to listen to the music itself in all its paradoxical profusion.

SHOSTAKOVICH AT THE PROMS
For a full list of Shostakovich's music being performed at this year's Proms, see the Index of Works, pages 156–9
• See also Proms Films, page 120

'I am not dead; although buried in the earth, I live on in you, whose lamentations I can hear, since friend is reflected in friend …'

Lines by Michelangelo, set by Shostakovich in 1974, the year before his death

RIGHT
Taking refuge in the privacy of music: Shostakovich at a rehearsal in the Moscow Conservatoire, c1962

Celebrating Mozart's 250th Year and his Opera Legacy on Arthaus DVD VIDEO™

100 012 - Picture Format: 16:9

Così Fan Tutte

An "utterly ravishing" *(Opera Now)* 2000 production from the Zürich Opera House sees Bartoli make her debut as Fiordiligi, under the distinguished musical direction of Nikolaus Harnoncourt.

100 328 - Picture Format: 16:9

Don Giovanni

Rodney Gilfry and Cecilia Bartoli lead a first rate group of singers in a 2001 staging which reunites director Jürgen Flimm with Bartoli, Harnoncourt and the forces of the Zürich Opera House following the superb critical success of *Così* (100 012).

100 406 - Picture Format: 4:3

La Clemenza di Tito

Nicholas Hytner's critically-acclaimed and elegant staging, conducted by Andrew Davis and performed in the original Italian, comes from the 1991 Mozart Bicentenary season at Glyndebourne. The formidable cast is led by Philip Langridge, Ashley Putnam and Diana Montague.

102 007 - Picture Format: 4:3

La Finta Giardiniera

"This production of *La Finta Giardiniera* at the Drottningholm Court Theatre... proved not only an evening of rare enchantment, but an instructive argument for period performance of Mozart."
(The Independent)

100 002 - Picture Format: 16:9

Le Nozze di Figaro

Mozart's irresistible opera receives a sparkling 1999 performance: "one of the most acclaimed interpretations of recent years" *(amazon.co.uk)*; "this is nothing less than a consummate Figaro... an ensemble of surpassing musicality, acting skills, and sheer charismatic stage presence."
(culturevulture.net)

100 188 - Picture Format: 4:3

Die Zauberflöte

This 1992 production by Axel Manthey combines an exquisite simple staging and gorgeous colourful costumes with superb casting, featuring some of today's leading Mozart singers: "this Flute is a gem."
(Classics Today)

Also available is the midprice range from Arthaus (φ), presenting classic 1970s and 1980s Glyndebourne opera at a special lower price.

This new Mozart boxset showcases six operas, also available individually: *Così Fan Tutte* (101 081), *Don Giovanni*, (101 087), *Die Entführung aus dem Serail* (101 091), *Idomeneo* (101 079), *Le Nozze di Figaro* (101 089) and *Die Zauberflöte* (101 085).

BBC SINGERS

Chief Conductor Stephen Cleobury
Principal Guest Conductor Bob Chilcott
Associate Composer Judith Bingham

"Not many small choirs
exhibit the easy virtuosity of
the BBC Singers"
Financial Times, October 2005

"The brilliant BBC Singers –
... the SAS of choirs"
Sunday Times, November 2005

"Sensational ... the BBC
Singers gave a lesson in class,
strength and vocal virtuosity"
El País, December 2005

For more information about forthcoming
concerts, or to join the Friends of the
BBC Singers:

Tel 020 7765 1862
Email singers@bbc.co.uk
bbc.co.uk/singers

For all other enquiries, call 020 7765 4370

BBC RADIO 3
90-93 FM

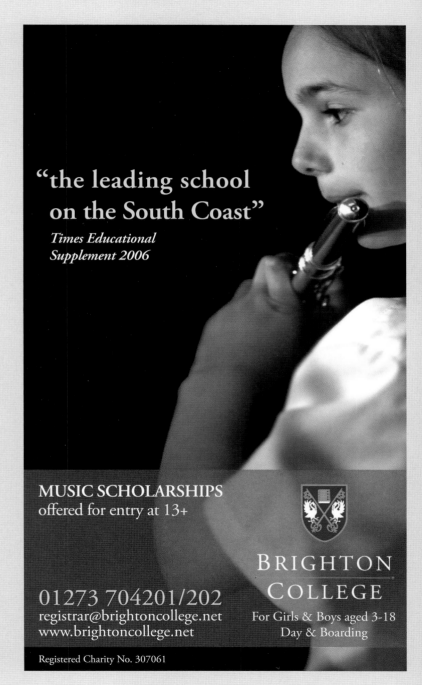

New MUSIC

Who's afraid of modern music? Just about everyone, it seems. But why be afraid, says **Paul Driver**, when the BBC Proms are there to be your listener-friendly guide …

If you write professionally about modern music, as I do, friends and acquaintances are apt to say – it can become the refrain of your life – that you really must publish a guidebook and 'tell us what it is all about'. This may seem a flattering request, but it is dispiriting for several reasons. First, it assumes that music from, in effect, Wagner to the present day is readily and actually summarisable. Second, it suggests that even people who find their bearings without much trouble in contemporary art, literature or cinema have insuperable problems with music; and third, it reveals that, in many cases, they aren't too bothered about the fact.

They are, perhaps generously, showing an interest in something that, if it passes them by, it passes them by. Not to know your ABC in music has not, in this country, been regarded as a disastrous cultural embarrassment, since music – especially the modern sort – is widely considered arcane. And though people who actively dislike modern music tend to do so with a stridency not directed at modern art or literature – perhaps because you can't walk away from a performance as easily as you can from a picture – it is from well-meaning indifference that modern music has had most to fear.

A conspiracy of silence

Contemporary composers do not often make the headlines or win high-profile prizes like the Booker or Turner, and they are seldom discussed on mainstream radio, still less television. Their marginalisation is altogether astonishing. And it is doubtful whether any guidebook, however handily readable, would make much difference, and not merely because people have to discover what matters to them for themselves. The music of the 20th and 21st centuries presents an unmanageably teeming phenomenon, even if you regard it only from the point of view of the western classical tradition.

One cannot 'tell' such a story in a slim volume, though one might do so in a quick paragraph or even parenthesis (listen to Wagner's *Tristan und Isolde* followed by Debussy's *Pelléas et Mélisande*, Schoenberg's Five Orchestral Pieces, Berg's *Wozzeck* and Webern's Symphony, then consider Stravinsky's *The Rite of Spring* followed by his cantata *Les noces*, and apprise yourself of Bartók's ballet *The Miraculous Mandarin* and his last three string quartets, move on to Messiaen's *Oiseaux exotiques*, back to Britten's *Peter Grimes*, on again to Boulez's *Le marteau sans maître*, seeking amplification of the latter's linguistic reforms in Stockhausen's tri-orchestral *Gruppen*, and, having pondered Maxwell Davies's orchestral *Second Taverner Fantasia*, Birtwistle's orchestral *Earth Dances* and Elliott Carter's *Symphony of Three Orchestras*, pause for breath).

No, to savour the full richness of this overwhelmingly beautiful repertoire that, in Ezra Pound's formulation, is 'news that stays news',

JULIAN ANDERSON
(born 1967)
Heaven is Shy of Earth
BBC commission: world premiere
PROM 32

GEORGE BENJAMIN
(born 1960)
Dance Figures
UK premiere
PROM 14

PROMS COMPOSER PORTRAIT
SEE PAGE 48

SIR PETER MAXWELL DAVIES
(born 1934)
A Little Birthday Music
BBC commission: world premiere
PROM 7

JAMES DILLON
(born 1950)
Piano Concerto
BBC commission: world premiere
PROM 36

DAI FUJIKURA
(born 1977)
Crushing Twister
*BBC commission:
world premiere*
PROM 58

there is only one sound remedy. Go to the Proms! By some amazing chance, the guidebook I find so elusive is being written in tones in the air, from summer to summer, at the Royal Albert Hall. Here connections are drawn, contexts proliferate, and a forum for today's composers exists that genuinely reaches a large public – a global one, indeed – and seems uniquely able to persuade people to put music at the forefront of their minds.

Music that looks forward

This year six works have been specially commissioned by the BBC, including two for the Proms Chamber Music series, while 13 more pieces receive their world, European, UK or London premieres. In addition, half a dozen or so other living composers are represented, two or three recently deceased ones, and a quantity of others from that post-Wagnerian (so-called 'modern') period that can still, apparently, so flummox today's concert-goers.

Yes, the name of Anton Webern can still cause alarm. But his orchestral Passacaglia, Op. 1 – given its UK premiere by Henry Wood at a 1931 Prom and to be heard again, 75 years later, in this season's Prom 16 – is an example of a scary-seeming work that turns out to be a pure lulling: a Brahmsian preamble to an oeuvre that never left Romantic rubato behind, for all its ascetic, newfangled classicism. Nor should Morton Feldman's *Rothko Chapel* (Prom 63) drive the dissonance-averse listener screaming from the hall. It, too, is a music of calm, a litany of leisurely vocal (wordless) and instrumental phrases, and Feldman's work

in general counts among the last century's most pacific musical achievements as well as its most radical. Avoiding stylistic trends, even the minimalism to which he might seem close, Feldman devised a music of matt blandness that is somehow totally compelling; exemplary, I like to think, for the coming times.

This season one can encounter works by such 20th-century masters as the Polish Witold Lutoslawski (Prom 45), who reinvigorated symphonic style with a dose of the 'chance operations' he learnt from the music of John Cage; the German Hans Werner Henze (Proms 25 and 60), who has made eclecticism a healthy way of life; the Russian Alfred Schnittke (Proms 39 and 47, and PSM 1), who lifted it to a new expressive plateau and called it 'polystylistics'; and the Hungarian György Ligeti (Prom 9), whose micro-attentiveness to part-writing has created an instantly recognisable sound-world, familiar from the film *2001: A Space Odyssey*. Outstanding 20th-century composers have often developed such sonic 'brands', and the American Steve Reich (Prom 37) is no exception. His type of minimalism is unmistakable from the first bar of any piece, though that of his younger compatriot John Adams (Prom 38) is likely to be disguised in one of various ways.

The Finnish Magnus Lindberg, whose recent *Sculpture* has its UK premiere (Prom 55), is a case in point. By activating what the conductor Esa-Pekka Salonen has called the 'computer in his head', he generates vast streams of notes and directs them into constantly intriguing forms, a sort of liquid sculpture (for the structures never have time to solidify) that is absolutely distinctive every time. That teeming character of 20th-century

DETLEV GLANERT (born 1960)
Four Preludes and Serious Songs
(after Brahms)
UK premiere
PROM 19

OSVALDO GOLIJOV
(born 1960)
Three Songs
UK premiere
PROM 54

HK GRUBER
(born 1943)
Hidden Agenda
UK premiere
PROM 52

JONATHAN HARVEY
(born 1939)
... towards a Pure Land
London premiere
PROM 35
PROMS COMPOSER PORTRAIT
SEE PAGE 48

HANS WERNER HENZE
(born 1926)
Five Messages for the
Queen of Saba
London premiere
PROM 60

music seems to be emblematised here. Like James Dillon, whose new Piano Concerto (Prom 36) is a follow-up Proms commission to his Violin Concerto of 2000, and whose work similarly suggests that notes are a kind of ductile or malleable force, Lindberg makes you aware of the wonderful liberation of means that was 20th-century music, without looking nostalgically back.

Music that looks back

The Austrian HK Gruber, on the other hand, has made a speciality of the backward look. His remarkable series of concertos (not least the one for trumpet, *Aerial*, a BBC commission premiered at the Proms in 1999) and more recently his chamber-orchestral *Timescapes* and orchestral *Dancing in the Dark* (given its UK premiere at the 2003 Proms) combine a secret, even Schoenbergian and constructivistic rigour of workmanship with a frank evocation of light music: the sentimental pop song that emerges at the end of his First Violin Concerto, Viennese cabaret in the Cello Concerto, or the Roaring Twenties dance-band mimicry in *Timescapes*. As for *Frankenstein!!* (Prom 52), his Gothic 'pan-demonium' for chansonnier and orchestra, it is entirely and wildly parodic, yet the strength of the structure is never in doubt. In that tension between nostalgia and scaffolding lie both the charm and profundity of Gruber's music. It is not surprising that his new orchestral work (also Prom 52) should be called – and have a – *Hidden Agenda*.

Ironic reflection of popular idioms has long been associated with Sir Peter Maxwell Davies, and in his new role as Master of the Queen's Music he is certainly not above excoriating us with pastiche. Because his Proms commission for children's choirs and the BBC Symphony Orchestra (Prom 7) is an 80th-birthday tribute to the Queen – to a specially written text by the Poet Laureate, Andrew Motion – it is unlikely to lash out, but one can't be sure. Mark-Anthony Turnage, too, is fond of the strains of the past: his *A Relic of Memory* (receiving its UK premiere in Prom 53) takes its starting-point from Bach's *St Matthew Passion*, while also incorporating his own choral elegy *Calmo* (a BBC commission for the 2004 Proms).

Music of many worlds

Eclecticism is not necessarily the way forward, even if it is the way back, but for composers who voraciously feed the folk musics of the world into their work, such as the Argentine-born Osvaldo Golijov (whose *Three Songs* have their UK premiere in Prom 54), it has become as much a true path as the avant-garde approach of Boulez and Stockhausen was once seen to be. Among the younger generation, Julian Anderson stands interestingly in both camps, writing folkish and flaringly exotic pieces that are well versed in the procedures of post-war modernism, electronics included. His thoroughness is shown, too, by the fact that he troubled to join a symphony chorus before tackling his Prom commission for this year, *Heaven is Shy of Earth*, a set of choral-orchestral settings of Emily Dickinson and texts from the Latin Mass (Prom 32).

TOSHIO HOSOKAWA
(born 1955)
Circulating Ocean
UK premiere
PROM 27

PROMS COMPOSER PORTRAIT
SEE PAGE 48

HANSPETER KYBURZ
(born 1960)
Noesis
London premiere
PROM 64

MAGNUS LINDBERG
(born 1958)
Sculpture
UK premiere
PROM 55

PROMS COMPOSER PORTRAIT
SEE PAGE 48

COLIN MATTHEWS
(born 1946)
Animato; Scorrevole
BBC commission: world premiere
PCM 7

WOLFGANG RIHM
(born 1952)
Verwandlung
UK premiere
PROM 18

Past and present going hand in hand

The modernist mainstream, if still flowing, can be traced in Germany to Wolfgang Rihm and Matthias Pintscher, and in this country to George Benjamin, Jonathan Harvey and possibly Colin Matthews. New works by all of them can be heard this season, as will some of the seductive orchestral arrangements of Debussy's piano *Préludes* that Matthews originally made for the Hallé (Prom 64). Matthews, of course, is a contemporary composer who did make the headlines – even the *Nine O'Clock News* – when, in the year 2000, he added a new movement, 'Pluto', to Holst's *The Planets*. Two years earlier, Anthony Payne's 'elaboration' of Elgar's unfinished Third Symphony (commissioned by the BBC back in 1932) had created even more of a worldwide stir, and his new completion of the same composer's *Pomp and Circumstance* March No. 6 (receiving its world premiere in Prom 26) is almost bound to excite similarly widespread press and popular interest. What with Detlev Glanert expanding his orchestration of Brahms's *Four Serious Songs* to embrace four new Preludes and a Postlude of his own (Prom 19), perhaps such surrogate existence will be increasingly what classical composers can hope for in these difficult times. One wonders how the future must seem to one of the youngest composers mentioned here, the British-based Dai Fujikura, whose commission for the BBC Concert Orchestra is unveiled in Prom 58. One thing is sure, though. Thanks to the Proms, the prospects for new music, and its wider appreciation, are hugely enhanced.

YOUNG COMPOSERS COMPETITION 2006
IF YOU CREATE IT, WE WANT TO HEAR IT!

FOR FULL RULES, INFORMATION AND **GREAT PRIZES** PLEASE VISIT
www.bbc.co.uk/proms

The BBC Proms/Guardian Young Composers Competition is a unique opportunity for creative and talented young composers who want to be inspired to write more.

*The*Guardian

BBC PROMS

STEVEN STUCKY
(born 1949)
Second Concerto for Orchestra
UK premiere
PROM 41

MARK-ANTHONY TURNAGE
(born 1960)
A Relic of Memory
UK premiere
PROM 53

BENJAMIN WALLFISCH
(born 1979)
New work
world premiere
PSM 4

IAN WILSON
(born 1964)
Red Over Black
BBC co-commission with the Royal Philharmonic Society: world premiere
PCM 5

Proms Composer Portraits
In the Royal Albert Hall

PCP 1 George Benjamin (5.30pm, before Prom 14)
PCP 2 Toshio Hosokawa (5.00pm, before Prom 27)
PCP 3 Jonathan Harvey (5.30pm, before Prom 35)
PCP 4 Magnus Lindberg (5.30pm, before Prom 55)

Each composer will discuss the new work being performed in the main evening Prom and introduce live performances of selected chamber-scale pieces (see main Proms listings for details). *Free tickets available at Door 6 from 30 minutes beforehand. Latecomers will not be admitted until a suitable break in the performance. Proms Composer Portraits will be recorded for broadcast on BBC Radio 3 immediately after that day's main evening Prom.*

PROMS COMPOSER PORTRAITS

GLYNDEBOURNE
ON TOUR 2006

W A MOZART
COSÌ FAN TUTTE
A new production directed by Nicholas Hytner,
premiered at the 2006 Festival

J STRAUSS II
DIE FLEDERMAUS
A revival of Stephen Lawless's production,
premiered at the 2003 Festival

B BRITTEN
THE TURN OF THE SCREW
A new production for the 2006 Tour, directed by Jonathan Kent

GLYNDEBOURNE	10 – 28 October
WOKING	31 October – 4 November
PLYMOUTH	7 – 11 November
MILTON KEYNES	14 – 18 November
NORWICH	21 – 25 November
STOKE-ON-TRENT	28 November – 2 December
SADLER'S WELLS	5 – 9 December

To join our FREE mailing list and receive full details for the 2006 Tour,
please call 01273 815 000 or email info@glyndebourne.com
or write to: GOT Mailing List, Freepost BR (235), Glyndebourne,
Lewes, East Sussex BN8 4BR

www.glyndebourne.com

GLYNDEBOURNE ON TOUR...
A YOUTHFUL AND VIBRANT JOURNEY
Sunday Independent 2000

New HORIZONS

Lincoln Abbotts, Proms Learning Consultant, surveys the many ways in which the BBC is expanding the experience of live music-making to new audiences across the country

With 73 concerts at the Royal Albert Hall, many of which are televised and all of which are broadcast live on BBC Radio 3 and online, the Proms already play a pivotal role in introducing classical music to a huge new audience. Our learning programme sits at the core of this intense two months of musical activity, offering opportunities for families and musicians, both young and old, amateur and professional, to become involved in the experience of live music-making.

Times have changed. Today's educational landscape is remarkably diverse and our musical culture is becoming ever more pluralistic. Through its learning initiatives, the BBC aims to support and explore the skills, processes and approaches needed for musicians working in our exciting, ever-evolving culture.

The BBC's own performing groups – the BBC orchestras, choruses and the BBC Singers – have always played a central role within the Proms and learning is now part of their core remit. In recent years literally thousands of children and their families have enjoyed their first taste of live orchestral music through Radio 3's *Making Tracks Live* concerts, as well as workshops in schools and with community groups around the UK.

Variously the BBC has mounted projects inspired by football, supermarkets, violas, the music of Iran and Urban Grime.

The BBC Proms can boast an equally innovative track record. Our *Out+About* concerts present the visceral excitement of an orchestra at close quarters to thousands of families each year; through *Music Intro* other families have been introduced for the very first time to orchestras and the music they play; while our flagship creative project of 2005 – the Proms *Violins!!* day – brought together star violinist Viktoria Mullova and world-class professionals from the BBC Symphony Orchestra with the contemporary music ensemble Between The Notes and aspiring young musicians from Southampton, Cheltenham, Berkshire and Gateshead.

Going out

Staying in may well be the new going out, but the Proms have always challenged trends and conventions. Our flagship creative project this year is all about *The Voice*. This cross-border collaboration is in equal measure about encouraging those in Glasgow and London who already sing to try something new and enticing those who don't already sing, but think they might like to, to take part in creating and performing a brand-new piece for Proms 20 and 21.

Under the creative inspiration of composer/choral director Orlando Gough, co-founder of The Shout (hailed by *The Times* as 'a blueprint for 21st-century choral singing'), and with a text by Caryl Churchill that focuses on climate change, it's a frisky venture involving upwards of 1,000 massed voices drawn from youth choirs based both north and south of

LEFT
All ears: eager young Prommers attending a Blue Peter Prom

RIGHT
Expanding their horizons: both young musicians and seasoned orchestral players learnt to play the Iranian *daf* during the BBC Symphony Orchestra's 'Persepolis' week

Variously the BBC has mounted projects inspired by football, supermarkets, violas, the music of Iran and Urban Grime.

the border, as well as the BBC Symphony Chorus and Huddersfield Choral Society, with members of the BBC Symphony Orchestra and BBC Scottish Symphony Orchestra providing accompaniment. To add to the whole sublime noise, there'll also be 'Rabble Choirs' made up of singers-to-be from Glasgow and London, as well as a Prommers' Rabble, with members of The Shout acting as rabble-rousers *(see pages 70–71).*

Side-by-side

All the BBC's performing groups run 'side-by-side' initiatives – it's such an effective way of offering young players inspiration, encouragement and possible routes in to new repertoire and ways of working. Sitting alongside a professional orchestral musician, sharing a music-stand (and maybe a cup of tea), observing how a conductor gets the best results within a finite rehearsal time – it's all invaluable experience for youngsters who aspire to make their living as professional musicians.

Additionally, this year's two Blue Peter Proms (Proms 10 and 12) will see young Music Makers recruited from across the country joining the BBC Philharmonic on stage at the Royal Albert Hall to play Murray Gold's new version of the programme's familiar theme tune.

For one night only

Our *Out+About* events in 2006 will build on the huge success of past visits to the Brixton Academy (2003), Hammersmith Town Hall and the Hackney Empire (2004) and Alexandra Palace (2005). On Friday 16 June, the BBC Symphony Orchestra, together with the Proms and Radio 3

Making Tracks production teams, will be heading out to the Hexagon Theatre, Reading, for two concerts – one for 7- to 11-year-olds, followed by an evening invitation to families from across Reading and the Thames Valley to experience at first hand live classical music of the highest quality. Big screens, lively lighting and engaging presentation will all add to the power and potency of an orchestra in full flow.

Write here, right now

The mantra of our Guardian/BBC Proms Young Composers Competition is 'If you create it, we want to hear it'. And the 'it' can be hip-hop, jazz, string quartet or some new genre as yet unnamed. This freedom to explore and to experiment, to learn and to push at the boundaries, is a reflection of the entrepreneurial spirit that's out there among today's young musicians. Independent and imaginative, at ease with technology and multiple influences, they are the Creatives of the future and we want to support and encourage them.

As well as a chance to hear the winning competition entries in our annual Young Composers Concert (before Prom 38), this year sees the introduction of *Inspire* – a day of creative music-making which the young composers will spend with workshop pioneer Peter Wiegold, Master of the Queen's Music Sir Peter Maxwell Davies and leading American composer John Adams, plus the musicians of the Endymion ensemble. It will be a very hands-on, practical day, unpacking the many and varied skills and the flexibility of approach needed by composers working today, at a time when their role is undergoing continual redefinition.

Sitting alongside a professional orchestral musician, sharing a music-stand, observing how a conductor gets the best results within a finite rehearsal time – it's all invaluable experience for youngsters who aspire to make their living as professional musicians.

ABOVE
Young Blue Peter Prommers queue up outside the Royal Albert Hall

LEFT & FAR RIGHT
Listen and learn: aspiring young musicians enjoy the shared experience of playing alongside older professionals in one of our 'side-by-side' initiatives

It's a family thing

Orchestras are made up of families. The ways in which the strings, winds, brass and percussion work together, and their relationship with a conductor in creating the dynamic that helps to make a concert really great, all find parallels in the way we live our own family lives.

During the 2005 Proms, *Music Intro* began exploring the notion of extended families working together – something more than just a children's workshop with parents looking on. *Music Intro* is now incorporated into the learning programmes of all the BBC orchestras and the scheme will continue to develop during this year's Proms, offering yet more families their first chance to experience some of the finest music-making in the world. A couple of reactions from last year's families say it all: 'The workshop was outstanding! Same again next year, please!' 'More, more, more!! We thoroughly enjoyed ourselves and we haven't even been to the concert yet!' In addition, there are extended pre-concert workshops open to all (see BBC Proms website for details).

Making the connection

What connects all these activities is the BBC's continuing commitment to finding fresh and innovative ways of encouraging new audiences to experience the thrill of live classical music. The BBC Proms learning portfolio is at the heart of this commitment.

ABOVE
Young drums: the Islington Drummers beat out a rhythm at a Blue Peter Prom

RIGHT
All together now: children and parents can share their first taste of live orchestral music thanks to the BBC's *Music Intro* scheme

'The workshop was outstanding! Same again next year, please!'

'More, more, more!! We thoroughly enjoyed ourselves and we haven't even been to the concert yet!'

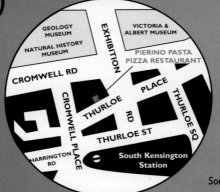

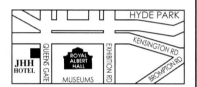

Meridian.
Your key to enjoyment.

One concept has informed and inspired Meridian Audio from the beginning, and it's a simple one: enjoyment.

Thus, the central focus of Meridian's internationally-acclaimed audio/video components, loudspeakers and systems is to enhance your enjoyment and quality of life, through home entertainment. Our goal is to help you enjoy the movies you watch more, and get more out of the music you listen to. Even the award-winning styling and appearance of Meridian products is designed to enhance your surroundings.

From a compact stereo system to a custom home theatre installation, the message is the same. When you're listening to music on a Meridian system, you are brought closer to it, and to the performers. We help recreate the space in which a performance takes place. Every nuance, subtlety and detail is clear. You hear and understand on a deeper level. You enjoy the music more.

Meridian brings you closer to the performance: closer to the heart of the art. A Meridian system is the ultimate enhancement for your lifestyle, enriching life and soul.

We recommend you experience Meridian enjoyment for yourself. Contact us to arrange a personal demonstration at your Meridian dealer.

BOOTHROYD STUART
MERIDIAN©

Meridian Audio Limited
Latham Road, Huntingdon, PE29 6YE, UK
Tel: +44 (0)1480 445678 Fax: +44 (0)1480 445686
www.meridian-audio.com/bpg/

CONCERT LISTINGS

The BBC: bringing the Proms to you – in concert, on radio, television and online

ADVANCE BOOKING

By post, fax and online *from Monday 15 May*

GENERAL BOOKING

In person, by phone or online *from Monday 12 June*

Telephone: 020 7589 8212
Online: bbc.co.uk/proms

For full booking information and postal/fax booking form *see pages 133–148*

PRICE CODES

A
▼
G

Each concert falls into one of seven different price bands, colour-coded for ease of reference. For full list of prices *see page 141* For special offers *see page 135*

NB: concert start-times vary across the season – check before you book

All concert details were correct at the time of going to press.
The BBC reserves the right to alter artist or programme details as necessary.

FOCUS ON … PROM I
MEET THE BBC SO'S NEW CHIEF CONDUCTOR

Jiří Bělohlávek launches our anniversary surveys of the music of Mozart and Shostakovich, and pays his own personal tribute to two composers from his own Czech homeland

When Jiří Bělohlávek raises his baton on this year's First Night of the Proms, he assumes his position as Chief Conductor of the BBC Symphony Orchestra. He also raises the curtain on this season's two major composer anniversaries – those of Mozart (born 250 years ago) and Shostakovich (born in 1906).

'It's a combination that works well,' says Bělohlávek. 'Not only because their musical characters are so different, but also because Shostakovich has nowadays gained a "classical" distinction within the symphonic tradition.'

Bělohlávek studied in Prague, where he became Music Director of the Czech Philharmonic before founding the Prague Philharmonia. Czech music is a natural area of expertise, so it is fitting that his opening programme includes both Bohemia's best-known musical export – the rippling riverscape 'Vltava' from Smetana's patriotic cycle *Má vlast* ('My Country') – and Dvořák's rarely heard, festive *Te Deum*. 'The *Te Deum* is a glorious piece but it is not so well known, and it's one of my happy goals to bring such neglected pieces out from the shadows of more famous works.'

As for Shostakovich's Fifth Symphony – offered up by the composer, following a public

damning in *Pravda*, as a 'Soviet Artist's Practical Creative Reply to Just Criticism' – Bělohlávek relishes it in purely musical terms. 'We know it was a sort of attempt at reconciliation after the harsh criticism, but I think the piece is also such an incredible composition, with great drama and wonderful setting for the orchestra. I think we can really see it as one of his best symphonies.'

ABOVE RIGHT
Dmitry Shostakovich
in the 1930s

RIGHT
Jiří Bělohlávek: new
Chief Conductor
of the BBC SO

PROM I
7.30pm – c9.50pm

Mozart
The Marriage of Figaro –
Overture; 'Porgi amor'   8'

Idomeneo – 'Oh smania! oh furie! …
D'Oreste, d'Aiace'   6'

Smetana
Má vlast – Vltava   12'

Dvořák
Te Deum   20'

interval

Shostakovich
Symphony No. 5 in D minor   50'

Barbara Frittoli *soprano*
Sir John Tomlinson *bass*

BBC Symphony Chorus
BBC Symphony Orchestra
Jiří Bělohlávek *conductor*

Czech maestro Jiří Bělohlávek (*see panel, left*) conducts his first First Night in a Proms triple celebration marking the launch of his tenure as the BBC SO's new Chief Conductor and of our season-long anniversary explorations of Mozart (born 1756) and Shostakovich (born 1906). Dvořák's *Te Deum* was the work with which the Czech composer launched his own new position as director of New York's National Conservatory of Music over 100 years ago; it joins his compatriot Smetana's ode to his Czech homeland.

Broadcast on BBC TWO

Proms Extras venue codes
RAH • Royal Albert Hall
WAF • West Arena Foyer, RAH
RGS • Royal Geographical Society

Every Prom live on BBC Radio 3 and bbc.co.uk/proms • Advance Booking from 15 May • General Booking from 12 June: 020 7589 8212

PROM 2

7.30pm – c9.45pm

Mozart the Dramatist

Idomeneo – ballet music	15'
Mitridate – 'Se viver non degg'io'	6'
Zaide – 'Nur mutig, mein Herze'	5'
Lucio Silla – 'Fra i pensier'	5'
The Abduction from the Seraglio – Act 2 Finale	10'
interval	
La clemenza di Tito – Overture	5'
Don Giovanni – 'Dalla sua pace'	4'
The Marriage of Figaro – scene from Act 3	10'
The Magic Flute – 'Ach, ich fühl's'	5'
Don Giovanni – Act 2 Finale	18'

Anna Leese soprano
Rebecca Nash soprano
Ailish Tynan soprano
Ian Bostridge tenor
Benjamin Hulett tenor
Simon Keenlyside baritone
Kyle Ketelsen bass-baritone
Brindley Sherratt bass

BBC Singers (men's voices)
Scottish Chamber Orchestra
Sir Roger Norrington conductor

A kaleidoscopic survey of the composer's
major stage works (see panel, right).

Recorded for broadcast on BBC ONE

🗩 **6.00pm Pre-Prom Talk** (RAH)
Sir Roger Norrington in conversation with
Nicholas Kenyon, Director of the Proms

FOCUS ON ... PROM 2

M IS FOR MOZART, MUSICIAN AND MAN OF THE THEATRE

Sir Roger Norrington masterminds a whistle-stop tour of most of Mozart's major operas,
demonstrating his dramatic genius in both aria and ensemble

It's right that any survey of Mozart's major dramatic output should begin with music from *Idomeneo*. For, although the composer wrote his first operatic score, *Apollo et Hyacinthus*, at the age of only 11, and enjoyed the huge honour of having his fourth opera, *Mitridate*, commissioned for the ducal theatre in Milan just three years later, it was only with the 1781 premiere of *Idomeneo* – the powerfully emotional tale of a father sworn to sacrifice his own son – that the 25-year-old Mozart finally revealed his true mastery of dramatic form and ability to create real flesh-and-blood characters, even out of the dusty figures of ancient Greek myth.

As Sir Roger Norrington observes, early operas such as *Mitridate* 'were really just suits for singers, tailor-made to their vocal demands. Character didn't come into it. But then, with *Idomeneo*, because he was older and had experienced more – both great things and setbacks – it all just clicked into place and he begins to show that unerring sense of character, and ability to put those characters into his music, which no-one else at the time, not even Haydn, possessed. So we get such wonderful things as the Act 3 sextet from *Figaro*, with all the characters popping out at you – and of course another stack of characters in the pit, with four woodwind jokers (five, if you count the horn) all ready to comment on everything that's going on!'

Sir Roger is particularly struck by the pattern outlined by the last seven operas, which go from *opera seria* (*Idomeneo*) to *singspiel* (*Seraglio*) to comedy (*Figaro*) to *dramma giocoso* (*Don Giovanni*), before 'running back down the ladder' from comedy (*Così*) to *singspiel* (*Magic Flute*) to *opera seria* again (*Clemenza di Tito*). 'So they form a symmetrical arch, with *Don Giovanni* – the most sinful, the most frightening – at its peak. It's as if he's touched lightning in *Don Giovanni* and then, too scared to try it again, runs back the way he's come to the safety of *opera seria*.' Fitting, then, that our survey should not just begin with *Idomeneo* but end with the hellfire finale of *Don Giovanni* too.

Proms Saturday Matinee
3.00pm Cadogan Hall

London Mozart Players
Isabelle van Keulen violin/director

Music by Mozart and Schnittke

See pages 108–9

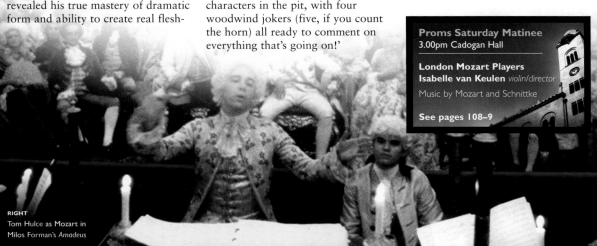

RIGHT
Tom Hulce as Mozart in
Milos Forman's *Amadeus*

Every Prom live on BBC Radio 3 and bbc.co.uk/proms • Advance Booking from 15 May • General Booking from 12 June: 020 7589 8212

61

WAGNER: SIEGFRIED

John Deathridge hails the heroic virtues of Wagner's dragon-slayer

The first complete cycle of Wagner's epic *Der Ring des Nibelungen* ('The Nibelung's Ring') at the Bayreuth festival theatre in the summer of 1876 was a major artistic and historical event. *Siegfried* in particular, the third drama in the cycle, turned out to be a huge success. By general agreement, here at his best was the composer who could conjure sounds never heard before from the orchestra and combine song with expressive instrumental writing to touch the deepest and most wonderful feelings in his audience. Even Eduard Hanslick, the most formidable of Wagner's critics, confessed his astonishment at discovering the work's 'freshness' of tone, its realism and the natural boyishness of its hero. Apart from such well-known extracts as the forging songs and the

'Forest Murmurs', *Siegfried* has proved less popular since then, unjustifiably so. It can be disconcerting. The tenor in the title-role has to face a newly-awakened, fresh-voiced Brünnhilde at the end after already singing on stage for hours. And Wagner brought to *Siegfried* an austerity hitherto unheard of in opera: brittle, facet-like orchestration that can disintegrate and recombine like the fragments of Siegmund's sword; a total absence of ensembles and choruses; and the deliberate paring down of the action to a very few characters.

But *Siegfried* is still wonderfully expressive and surprisingly modern in the way it refuses to cover up the fantasies of power enshrined in its hero. Nietzsche's 'superman' derives from him; and today's popular images of Superman (aka Clark Kent) are not far off. Siegfried is a disconcertingly gauche boy of the woods, yet miraculously able to confront evil with his innate superpowers, among other things by effortlessly killing a dragon, beheading one of his enemies and getting his woman in the end in true comic-book fashion. Thomas Mann called him a clown, a sun-god and an anarchist revolutionary all in one. *Siegfried* is heroic fiction at its best and most allusive, and one of Wagner's most brilliant and powerful scores.

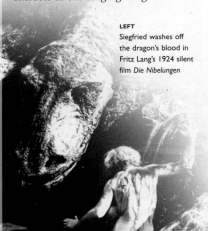

LEFT
Siegfried washes off the dragon's blood in Fritz Lang's 1924 silent film *Die Nibelungen*

PROM 3
4.00pm – c9.50pm

Wagner
Siegfried (concert performance; sung in German)   240'

Jon Fredric West *Siegfried*
Olga Sergeeva *Brünnhilde*
Evgeny Nikitin *Wanderer*
Volker Vogel *Mime*
Sergei Leiferkus *Alberich*
Mikhail Petrenko *Fafner*
Natalie Karl *Woodbird*
Qiu Lin Zhang *Erda*

Orchestre de Paris
Christoph Eschenbach *conductor*

Jon Fredric West

Christoph Eschenbach conducts the third instalment of our Proms *Ring* cycle (see panel, left), featuring a cast drawn largely from Robert Wilson's production seen earlier this year at the Châtelet Theatre in Paris. American tenor Jon Fredric West makes his Proms debut in the title-role.

There will be two intervals of 60 and 25 minutes

💬 **2.30pm Pre-Prom Talk** (RAH)
Discover Wagner's *Siegfried* with John Deathridge, Professor of Music at King's College, London

---

PROM 4
7.00pm – c9.00pm

Debussy
La mer   24'

Colin Matthews
Horn Concerto   23'

interval

Sibelius
Symphony No. 1 in E minor   38'

Richard Watkins *horn*

Hallé
Mark Elder *conductor*

Colin Matthews's 60th birthday is marked with four Proms performances this year, beginning with his Horn Concerto, one of his most successful recent works played by the soloist who premiered it in 2001 (see also Proms 5, 64 and 73 and PCM 7). Mark Elder, who returns to preside over this year's Last Night, also conducts Debussy's surging orchestral seascape and Sibelius's first foray into symphonic form.

♪ **1.00pm Proms Chamber Music**
See pages 110–13

💬 **5.30pm Pre-Prom Talk** (RGS)
Colin Matthews discusses his Horn Concerto with broadcaster Sarah Walker

---

Every Prom live on BBC Radio 3 and bbc.co.uk/proms • Advance Booking from 15 May • General Booking from 12 June: 020 7589 8212

62

PROM 5

10.00pm – c11.20pm

Jonathan Dove
Figures in the Garden .... 17'

Colin Matthews
To Compose Without the Least
Knowledge of Music .... 4'

Mozart
Serenade in B flat major, K361
'Gran Partita' .... 47'

London Winds
Michael Collins director/clarinet

Michael Collins

'It seemed to me that I was hearing the voice of God,' reminisces Mozart's rival Salieri over the sublime strains of the 'Gran Partita' in Milos Forman's film of Peter Shaffer's *Amadeus*. Fellow anniversarian Colin Matthews contributes his own wind-sextet realisation of Mozart's musical dice-game and, the night before Glyndebourne's annual visit, we hear Jonathan Dove's playfully allusive wind octet, commissioned for the Sussex opera festival's Mozart bicentenary season in 1991 and infused with the fragrance of its famous gardens and the memory of melodies from *The Marriage of Figaro*.

There will be no interval

PROM 6

6.30pm – c10.25pm

Mozart
Così fan tutte
(semi-staged; sung in Italian) .... 185'

Glyndebourne Festival Opera

Miah Persson *Fiordiligi*
Anke Vondung *Dorabella*
Topi Lehtipuu *Ferrando*
Luca Pisaroni *Guglielmo*
Nicolas Rivenq *Don Alfonso*
Ainhoa Garmendia *Despina*

Glyndebourne Chorus
Orchestra of the Age of Enlightenment
Iván Fischer conductor

Iván Fischer

Mozart's operatic masterpiece forms the operatic centrepiece of our 250th anniversary celebrations, in a semi-staging based on this summer's new Glyndebourne Festival production directed by Nicholas Hytner (*see panel, right*). Hungarian conductor Iván Fischer makes a welcome return to the Proms in his debut Glyndebourne season.

There will be one interval

🗨 **5.00pm Pre-Prom Talk** (RAH)
Discover Mozart's *Così fan tutte* with David Cairns, author of a new study of the composer's operas

FOCUS ON … PROM 6
MOZART: COSÌ FAN TUTTE

Rodney Milnes peers into the murky sexual waters of Mozart's most deceptively beautiful and emotionally confusing comedy

All great works of art change as time passes – or rather, our response to them does – and *Così fan tutte* has changed more than most. Throughout the 19th century it was considered trivial, unworthy of Mozart, and rarely performed. For much of the 20th century it was played just for laughs. Today it is recognised by many as formally, and indeed purely musically, the most perfect of all Mozart's operas, and one that can be profoundly disturbing.

It looks trivial on the surface: the plot is like that of a West End farce. Two young officers bet a cynical, older friend that their fiancées are models of fidelity. The friend hires the sisters' maid as an accomplice in deception. The officers pretend to go on active duty, but return in exotic disguise. After protesting their constancy in the first act, the sisters decide that a bit of fun with the two foreigners need not be out of the question. But they choose the 'wrong' partners – to the utter consternation of the men – and an instant double wedding is only interrupted by the officers' 'return' and the exposure of the fraud. *En route*, the waters get very muddy indeed: loyalty, trust, the whole nature of romantic love are thrown up in the air to the discomfiture of

RIGHT
Così fan tutte:
title-page of a 19th-century
piano reduction

all four (and of the audience).

The action has been seen as misogynist but, compared to the men's taking a bet on something so serious, the sisters' behaviour is surely pretty reasonable. Maybe the instant wedding is going a little far, but theatre conventions were different two centuries ago. However the piece ends – and the libretto leaves it open – the relationship of the sisters will survive, but after their display of macho competitiveness the men will surely never be able to face each other again.

Talking of changing conventions, in the 21st century it is possible to wonder, in the moments when the newly paired couples are off stage, whether in Alan Bennett's immortal words 'docking procedure' takes place. Add the element of physical sex, unthinkable in the 18th century, and the muddy waters get a great deal muddier.

Every Prom live on BBC Radio 3 and bbc.co.uk/proms • Advance Booking from 15 May • General Booking from 12 June: 020 7589 8212

63

FOCUS ON ... PROM 7

HAPPY BIRTHDAY, MA'AM!

Roderic Dunnett introduces the musical birthday present that the Poet Laureate and Master of the Queen's Music have written for Her Majesty

In one of the first collaborations between Poet Laureate and Master of the King's (or Queen's) Music since Ben Jonson and Nicholas Lanier produced masques for King James I, the current incumbents, Andrew Motion and Sir Peter Maxwell Davies (familiarly known as 'Max'), have teamed up for the first time to create a brand-new cantata, *A Little Birthday Music*, to be performed in the presence of HM The Queen and The Duke of Edinburgh in honour of Her Majesty's 80th birthday.

The problem with such commissions, admits Motion (whose annual salary is still the traditional 'butt of sherry sack'), is often just coming up with the initial idea. 'But Max proved the perfect collaborator: instantly when I asked him, he came up with just one word, "Constancy"; and that set ideas jostling and gave me the impetus for shaping the poem. What I've tried to create is a mixture of images, so as to give Max plenty to get his teeth into. But I haven't coloured the words too much, so as to leave room for his music to fill in the rest. I also tried to hint at some suggestion of a "green" future, which I know is an issue close to Max's heart.'

Max first set Motion's poem, *The Golden Rule*, as an anthem with organ accompaniment, to be sung at a service in St George's Chapel, Windsor, on St George's Day, two days after the Queen's actual 80th birthday. But for the Proms he's created a quite different setting to be performed by the BBC Symphony Orchestra, a fanfare of brass players from the Scots Guards

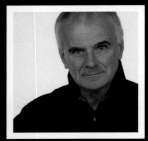

Band and some 250 children drawn from choirs across the country.

'Max' has long made a point of composing for children, both in his adopted Orkney and south of the border. Not that he's ever believed in making things too easy for them. 'It's absolutely vital not to write down to children. Instead, you try to ensure that the music will challenge and extend them. The hushed refrain – *The golden rule, your constancy, survives* – is really very tricky to pull off. Above all you want to make sure that everyone has total confidence in what they're doing.'

He's pretty confident himself that the brass of the Scots Guards Band will make a suitably ceremonial impact – 'and I'm sure those plucky young singers will let rip and fire from the hip!' So it should all go with a bang? 'Well, I think you could say it ends slightly on the loud side!'

ABOVE RIGHT
Music and words:
Sir Peter Maxwell Davies
and Andrew Motion

LEFT
Her Majesty – escorted by
Nicholas Kenyon, Director
of the Proms – meeting
Royal Albert Hall ushers on
her last visit to the Proms,
in Jubilee Year 2003

PROM 7

7.00pm – c9.35pm

A concert for the 80th birthday of HM The Queen

Sir Peter Maxwell Davies
A Little Birthday Music   c20'
BBC commission: world premiere

Mozart
Clarinet Concerto in A major, K622   30'

interval

Dvořák
Symphony No. 9 in E minor,
'From the New World'   45'

Julian Bliss *basset clarinet*

Choristers of the Chapels Royal, St James's Palace & Hampton Court Palace • City of Birmingham Symphony Youth Chorus • Children's International Voices of Enfield • Finchley Children's Music Group • New London Children's Choir • Southend Boys' & Girls' Choirs • Trinity Boys' Choir

Fanfare Trumpeters of the Scots Guards
BBC Symphony Orchestra
Jiří Bělohlávek *conductor*

To celebrate Her Majesty's 80th birthday, the Master of the Queen's Music and the Poet Laureate have collaborated on a new work for massed children's voices (see *panel, left*). Teenage virtuoso Julian Bliss (who played at the Jubilee Year 'Prom at the Palace') marks Mozart's 250th and the BBC SO's new Chief Conductor offers one of the most popular pieces from his Czech homeland.

Recorded for later broadcast on BBC ONE

5.00pm Pre-Prom Talk (RGS)
Sir Peter Maxwell Davies with John Evans

PROM 8
7.30pm – c9.40pm

Prokofiev
War and Peace – Overture   5'

Shostakovich
Suite on Verses by Michelangelo
Buonarroti   40'

interval

Prokofiev
Romeo and Juliet – excerpts   49'

Ildar Abdrazakov bass

BBC Philharmonic
Gianandrea Noseda conductor

Gianandrea Noseda

Principal Guest Conductor at the Mariinsky Theatre in St Petersburg as well as Principal Conductor of the BBC Philharmonic, Gianandrea Noseda presents an all-Russian programme that also taps into his Italian roots. Prokofiev's opera on Tolstoy's epic was posthumously premiered in Florence, while his vibrant Shakespearian ballet recounts the doomed love of Verona's most romantic couple. Shostakovich's late settings of Michelangelo sonnets were written to mark the 500th anniversary of the great Italian painter-poet.

🔊 **6.00pm Pre-Prom Talk** (RAH)
A Sixteenth Symphony? Composer Gerard McBurney introduces Shostakovich's *Suite on Verses by Michelangelo Buonarroti*

PROM 9
7.30pm – c9.30pm   **Wp**

György Ligeti
Ramifications   9'

Schumann
Symphony No. 4 in D minor
(original version)   30'

interval

Brahms
Violin Concerto in D major   42'

Northern Sinfonia
Thomas Zehetmair conductor/violin

Following their thrilling performance at last year's 'Violins!!' day, Thomas Zehetmair and his Northern Sinfonia return in a programme that contrasts the nocturnal landscape of Hungarian composer György Ligeti's *Ramifications* with the more Romantic expression of Brahms's Violin Concerto – whose gypsy-influenced finale itself carries a Hungarian flavour. And we launch our celebration of Schumann's 150th anniversary with his Fourth Symphony, performed in the original version preferred by his great friend and champion, Brahms *(see panel, right)*.

Thomas Zehetmair

🔊 **6.00pm Pre-Prom Talk** (RGS)
Broadcaster and critic Stephen Johnson introduces the original version of Schumann's Fourth Symphony

FOCUS ON ... PROM 9
SCHUMANN: SYMPHONY NO. 4

A century and a half after Schumann's death, **Misha Donat** welcomes a rare chance to hear his first thoughts on one of his most radical works

In 1841, the year after his marriage to Clara Wieck, Schumann made a concentrated effort to master the art of symphonic composition. In that one year alone he composed his 'Spring' Symphony (No. 1), an *Overture, Scherzo and Finale*, a single-movement *Fantasy* for piano and orchestra (later expanded into the Piano Concerto in A minor – see Prom 18), and a work described in Clara's diary as 'a symphony that should consist of one movement and yet contain an Adagio and Finale'. This one-movement symphony was premiered in Leipzig in 1841 but then lay gathering dust until Schumann revised it 10 years later and eventually published it, in 1853, restyled as a 'Symphonic Fantasy'. That later version – now known as the Fourth Symphony (the composer's next two symphonies having been issued in the meantime) – is the form in which it has mostly been played ever since. But it's good occasionally to hear the composer's first thoughts.

Certainly the revision managed to improve some of the music's thematic detail, particularly at transition-points, but the scoring is also considerably thicker. Schumann made the revision when he was unhappily employed as Music Director in Düsseldorf, and Brahms, who always preferred the less opaque original, was convinced that the many doublings of the melodic

lines were added in view of the unreliable quality of the Düsseldorf players. Brahms's insistence on having the 1841 score published caused a serious rift between him and Clara, who believed that her husband's last thoughts were sacrosanct. But, in whichever form it's heard, 150 years after Schumann's death his D minor Symphony remains a strikingly original work – one of the very first of its kind to forge the traditional four movements into a continuous and strongly unified whole.

BELOW
Double portrait of Robert and Clara Schumann, c1850

Every Prom live on BBC Radio 3 and bbc.co.uk/proms • Advance Booking from 15 May • General Booking from 12 June: 020 7589 8212

65

FOCUS ON ... PROM 11
MOZART x 2

Popular pianists Paul Lewis and Till Fellner make their Proms duo debut in the concerto that Mozart wrote to perform with his sister

RIGHT
Pianists x 2:
Till Fellner *(top)*
and Paul Lewis

Mozart didn't have much to be happy about when in January 1779 he returned, reluctantly, to Salzburg after failing to secure work in Germany, then in France. Worse still, his mother had died during the trip, and his relationship with his father had soured. Yet it was at this time that he wrote his concerto for two pianos, whose sunny outlook belies any anxieties over family or career, perhaps because it was written for Mozart to perform alongside his beloved sister Nannerl.

At this year's Proms it will be performed by a duo of young master pianists working together for the first time: UK-born Paul Lewis and the Austrian Till Fellner, both former pupils of Alfred Brendel.

Fellner recalls first meeting Lewis 'around 10 years ago, when we were having a lesson with Brendel on Beethoven's 'Emperor' Concerto: we'd take it in turns to accompany each other with the orchestral part. Now we try and get to each other's concerts whenever we can.'

For Lewis the equal difficulty of the two piano parts 'shows what an accomplished pianist Nannerl must have been'. And, he adds, 'It maybe doesn't have the greatness of Mozart's two minor-key concertos, but there's so much joy in the way it's put together.'

Fellner believes the two pianists will make a propitious match: 'I think Paul's musical view is that the composer comes first and not the interpreter, and that's exactly what I feel too.'

PROM 10
11.00am – c1.00pm

Blue Peter Prom – 'Safari'

Blue Peter presenters Zoë Salmon and Matt Baker let loose a musical menagerie in the Royal Albert Hall, with birds from Mozart's fantastical *The Magic Flute* and Stravinsky's Russian folk-tale ballet *The Firebird*, a cat courtesy of Aaron Copland, a whole collection of two- and four-legged creatures from Camille Saint-Saëns's *Carnival of the Animals*, music from *Wallace and Gromit* ... and even a real live Teddy from New Zealand (actually he's the singer!).

Zoë Salmon *presenter*
Matt Baker *presenter*
Chris Collins *special guest appearance*
Teddy Tahu Rhodes *baritone*

Islington Children's Music Group
BBC Philharmonic
Alexander Shelley *conductor*

Zoë Salmon

Matt Baker

Teddy Tahu Rhodes

PROM 11
7.30pm – c9.30pm

Janáček, ed. Mackerras
The Cunning Little Vixen – suite   20'

Mozart
Concerto in E flat major
for two pianos, K365   25'

interval

Dvořák
Symphony No. 7 in D minor   35'

Paul Lewis *piano*
Till Fellner *piano*

BBC National Orchestra of Wales
Richard Hickox *conductor*

Richard Hickox pairs two Czech works: a suite from Janáček's cartoon-strip opera about the adventures of a frisky young vixen and Dvořák's lyrical Seventh Symphony. Leading British and Viennese pianists Paul Lewis and Till Fellner perform together for the first time, continuing this year's Mozart festivities with the delightful concerto for two pianos *(see panel, left)*.

2.00pm Proms Film (RGS)
Ingmar Bergman's *The Magic Flute*.
See page 120

Every Prom live on BBC Radio 3 and bbc.co.uk/proms • Advance Booking from 15 May • General Booking from 12 June: 020 7589 8212

PROM 12

11.00am – c1.00pm

Blue Peter Prom – 'Safari'

Zoë Salmon *presenter*
Matt Baker *presenter*
Chris Collins *special guest appearance*
Teddy Tahu Rhodes *baritone*

Islington Children's Music Group
BBC Philharmonic
Alexander Shelley *conductor*

See Prom 10 for details

PROM 13

7.00pm – c9.00pm

Elgar
In the South (Alassio)   20'

Bliss
A Colour Symphony   32'

interval

Walton
Belshazzar's Feast   34'

Bryn Terfel *bass-baritone*

BBC National Chorus of Wales
London Symphony Chorus
Côr Caerdydd
London Brass
BBC National Orchestra of Wales
.... **x** *conductor*

Ever the champion of British music, Richard Hickox conducts his final Prom at the helm of the BBC NOW, ...ined by Welsh star ...yn Terfel and ...mbined choirs from ...he Old Testament .... Commissioned ...... — whose own In the ... written on holiday in Italy — Bliss's A Colour Symphony explores the heraldic associations of the colours purple, red, blue and green (see panel, right).

FOCUS ON … PROM 13
RICHARD HICKOX

The longtime champion of British music chooses an all-British programme for his last Prom as Principal Conductor of the BBC NOW

'I have always found it easier to write "dramatic" music than "pure" music. I like the stimulus of words, or a theatrical setting, a colourful occasion or the collaboration of a great player. There is only a little of the spider about me, spinning his own web from his inner being. I am more of a magpie type. I need what Henry James termed a *trouvaille* or a *donnée*.'

For Arthur Bliss, the stimulus for his *Colour Symphony* – commissioned at Elgar's suggestion for the Three Choirs Festival and premiered in Gloucester Cathedral in 1922 – came from a volume in a friend's library outlining the heraldic associations of various colours. Each of its four movements explores the meanings of a particular colour: purple's associations include pageantry and death; red recalls revelry, courage and magic; blue equates with deep water, skies, loyalty and melancholy; and green represents hope, joy, spring, victory.

'It's a really first-class piece,' believes Richard Hickox, who has chosen the work as the centrepiece of an all-British Prom marking his final appearance as Principal Conductor of the BBC National Orchestra of Wales. 'We've recently recorded it, so it's in the orchestra's blood.' Though he regards the symphony as representing Bliss's 'impressions' of the four colours, an open-air performance, floodlit in the relevant hues, was apparently a great success.

The concert culminates in Walton's *Belshazzar's Feast*, another early masterpiece from a composer who excelled at occasional pieces; and it opens with Elgar's overture *In the South*, 'one of his most pictorial and distinctive works,' says Hickox. 'Elgar wrote it in Italy and evokes in it the battles of Roman history. There's some of the most brutal music in all Elgar here, and some of the most elegiac too.'

Every Prom live on BBC Radio 3 and bbc.co.uk/proms • Advance Booking from 15 May • General Booking from 12 June: 020 7589 8212

67

FOCUS ON ... PROM 14
DAVID ROBERTSON

The BBC Symphony Orchestra's new Principal Guest Conductor recognises no musical barriers between the old and the new

California-born David Robertson recognises no musical boundaries. In the space of just two weeks in January he conducted the BBC Symphony Orchestra – of which he became Principal Guest Conductor this season – during its uncompromising Elliott Carter weekend and also fronted the orchestra's Mozart 250th-anniversary celebrations. With Haydn and Brahms placed alongside a UK premiere from George Benjamin, the first of his two Proms with the BBC SO this year is just as boundary-breaking.

Benjamin's *Dance Figures*, first heard in Chicago last year, was designed not only for concert use but also to be danced by the Brussels-based Rosas company. Does the music instantly suggest the need for dance? 'Certain numbers do,' says Robertson. 'In others, the dances move from being earthy to becoming stylised, in the sense of suggesting how the idea of dance might apply to many different metaphors, whether you're thinking of, say, light or birds – when clearly these can't really dance.'

Robertson first met Benjamin in 1992 while working on the premiere of his *Ringed by the Flat Horizon* and was struck by how 'his entire musical personality expresses itself in the way he views sound.' The seemingly unlikely combination of Benjamin with Haydn and Brahms is far from random. 'There's a certain Classical beauty in Benjamin's works,' says Robertson, 'that goes well with Haydn. I've placed Haydn alongside Benjamin a number of times: retroactively, people hear the Haydn differently from how they would have done before. Within that purity and Classical aspect there's also extraordinary energy and passion, which fits well with Brahms.'

Proms Composer Portrait
RAH, 5.30pm
(before Prom 14)

Before the UK premiere of his *Dance Figures* George Benjamin talks to Christopher Cook and performs a selection of his related *Piano Figures*, in an event that also includes another of his virtuosic chamber works, *Viola, Viola*.
See 'New Music', pages 44–8

RIGHT
The Rosas dance company in *Dance Figures*

PROM 14
7.30pm – c9.30pm

Haydn
Symphony No. 94 in G major, 'Surprise' — 21'

George Benjamin
Dance Figures — 17'
UK premiere

interval

Brahms
Piano Concerto No. 1 in D minor — 45'

Pierre-Laurent Aimard *piano*

BBC Symphony Orchestra
David Robertson *conductor*

Pierre-Laurent Aimard

Ending his first season as the BBC SO's new Principal Guest Conductor, American conductor David Robertson (*see panel, left*) leads a typically eclectic programme featuring a UK premiere from George Benjamin, Haydn's corrective for dozing audiences and Brahms's mighty First Piano Concerto, with the dazzling Pierre-Laurent Aimard as soloist.

♪ **1.00pm Proms Chamber Music**
See pages 110–13

♪ **5.30pm Composer Portrait** (RAH)
George Benjamin. See panel, left

PROM 15
7.30pm – c9.50pm

Rossini
The Barber of Seville – Overture;
'Cessa di più resistere' — 15'

Donizetti
L'elisir d'amore – 'Una furtiva lagrima' — 4'
La fille du régiment – 'Ah! mes amis' — 5'

Falla
Nights in the Gardens of Spain — 24'

interval

Falla
The Three-Cornered Hat – dances — 13'

Songs by **Gardel, Grever, Menéndez/Utrera, Monge** — 16'

Chabrier
España — 7'

Juan Diego Flórez *tenor*
Artur Pizarro *piano*

BBC Concert Orchestra
Barry Wordsworth *conductor*

Juan Diego Flórez

Sensational Peruvian tenor Juan Diego Flórez makes his Proms debut in *bel canto* arias and popular Latin American songs from his childhood. Portuguese pianist Artur Pizarro plays Falla's Andalusian nocturnes, and Barry Wordsworth ends a remarkable 16-year stint as Principal Conductor of the BBC Concert Orchestra.

❓ **5.45pm Proms Quiz** (RGS)
Stephanie Hughes quizzes Tasmin Little and other guest panellists. See the Proms website for details of how to submit your questions and win Proms tickets.
Recorded for broadcast on BBC Radio 3

Every Prom live on BBC Radio 3 and bbc.co.uk/proms • Advance Booking from 15 May • General Booking from 12 June: 020 7589 8212

68

PROM 16

7.00pm – c9.05pm

Webern
Passacaglia, Op. 1   11'

Shostakovich
Violin Concerto No. 1 in A minor   37'

interval

Brahms
Symphony No. 4 in E minor   42'

Leila Josefowicz *violin*

City of Birmingham Symphony Orchestra
Sakari Oramo *conductor*

Leila Josefowicz

The CBSO's dynamic Music Director returns with Proms favourite Leila Josefowicz for a trio of works linked by their use of the passacaglia form (a series of variations over a repeating bass pattern). Webern's *Passacaglia* was his graduation piece as a student of Schoenberg; Shostakovich's long-suppressed First Violin Concerto has a profound slow Passacaglia at its heart; and Brahms's last symphony ends in a series of 30 variations based on a chaconne theme from a Bach cantata.

🔊 **5.30pm Pre-Prom Talk** (RGS)
Leila Josefowicz discusses Shostakovich's Violin Concerto No. 1 with Sandy Burnett

---

PROM 17

10.15pm – c11.45pm

The Great Venetians

A sequence of polychoral motets and canzonas, concertato psalm settings and canticles, and virtuoso solo motets composed for the Basilica of St Mark's, 1570–1670, to include:

Giovanni Gabrieli
Plaudite omnis terra a 12   4'
Dulcis Iesu patris imago   7'

Monteverdi
Missa a 4 voci da cappella   21'
Laetatus sum a 5   6'

Cavalli
Salve regina a 3   9'

and works by **Grandi, Rovetta, Rigatti** and **Rosenmüller**

His Majestys Sagbutts & Cornetts
Monteverdi Choir
English Baroque Soloists
Sir John Eliot Gardiner *conductor*

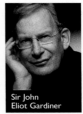
Sir John Eliot Gardiner

Sir John Eliot Gardiner presents a cross-section of sacred and secular music from the high point of Venice's musical history: a miscellany of psalms, motets and instrumental sonatas, transported in time and space from the heyday of La Serenissima to today's Royal Albert Hall (*see panel, right*).

There will be no interval

FOCUS ON ... PROM 17
GREAT VENETIANS

Tess Knighton sets the scene for Sir John Eliot Gardiner's sonorous salute to the sea-born city they called La Serenissima

The splendour of music-making in Venice in the 16th and 17th centuries reflected the apogee of the Venetian Republic's power as a trading port, a centre for advanced technology (such as printing) and a political force to be reckoned with. The soundworld of Venice was as colourful and magnificent as the paintings of Titian, Tintoretto and Veronese, as intricate and impressive as the mosaics adorning the interior of St Mark's. Sound became inextricably linked with the highly developed urban and liturgical ceremonial of the Republic and music intrinsic to the image of wealth, magnificence and power it wished to project.

St Mark's lay at the centre of all this musical activity, with a stream of famous composers and brilliant performers serving beneath its gilded domes. The Netherlander Adrian Willaert became *maestro di cappella* (choirmaster) in 1527, followed by Gioseffo Zarlino, Giovanni Croce, Claudio Monteverdi, Giovanni Rovetta and Francesco Cavalli, among others. The Gabrielis, Andrea and his nephew Giovanni, served as organists, and the composer Alessandro Grandi sang in the choir. These musicians also contributed to the soundscape of the city at large, including the many outdoor processions that heralded the presence of the Doge and the urban hierarchy.

Closely associated with the liturgical space of St Mark's is the tradition of the *cori spezzati*, the spatial grouping of singers and instrumentalists to perform the polychoral repertory through which music realised the sonorous magnificence so prized by the Doges. Even before Willaert, a Dutch pilgrim on his way to the Holy Land described the use of *cori spezzati* at St Mark's as 'altogether very beautiful and magnificent to hear and to see'. How much greater still was the impact, both visual and aural, of the concerted music later cultivated by the Gabrielis, the sheer virtuosity and brilliance of the tradition inspiring Monteverdi to the great and unforgettable psalm-settings of his *Vespers of 1610*.

Every Prom live on BBC Radio 3 and bbc.co.uk/proms • Advance Booking from 15 May • General Booking from 12 June: 020 7589 8212

69

PROM 18

7.30pm – c10.00pm

Wolfgang Rihm
Verwandlung   19'
UK premiere

Schumann
Piano Concerto in A minor   30'

interval

Mahler
Symphony No. 4 in G major   58'

Hélène Grimaud *piano*
Inger Dam-Jensen *soprano*

Bamberg Symphony Orchestra
Jonathan Nott *conductor*

Hélène Grimaud

Jonathan Nott, who has established a reputation as a leading British conductor abroad, brings his highly praised Bamberg orchestra to the Proms for an Austro-German concert featuring Schumann's powerful Piano Concerto performed by popular French pianist Hélène Grimaud. Inger Dam-Jensen offers the childlike vision of heavenly life that closes Mahler's Fourth Symphony. And Wolfgang Rihm's masterly and colourful *Verwandlung* explores the challenge of musical transformations.

🔊 **6.00pm Pre-Prom Talk** (RGS)
Wolfgang Rihm introduces his new work in conversation with Gillian Moore

PROM 19 ☐

8.00pm – c10.05pm

Brahms
Variations on the St Anthony Chorale 18'

Brahms/Glanert
Four Preludes and Serious Songs   25'
UK premiere

interval

R. Strauss
Ein Heldenleben   45'

Johan Reuter *bass-baritone*

BBC Scottish Symphony Orchestra
Marc Albrecht *conductor*

Marc Albrecht

'I find myself quite as interesting as Napoleon or Alexander,' Strauss once quipped as justification for making himself the subject of his large-scale tone-poem *A Hero's Life*, and he also made sure to include 'lots of horns', which, he added, 'are always a yardstick of heroism'. Brahms's expansion of a theme once thought to be by Haydn is matched by an expansion of Brahms's own *Four Serious Songs* by Detlev Glanert, whose *Theatrum bestiarum* enjoyed a successful premiere here last year.

🔊 **6.30pm Pre-Prom Talk** (RGS)
Detlev Glanert introduces his new work in conversation with Andrew Kurowski

PROM 20 ➡ ☐

2.30pm – c4.40pm

The Voice I
Orlando Gough
Open   3'
world premiere

Gershwin
An American in Paris   18'

A cappella choral works by
Hovhaness, Thea Musgrave
and **Steven Sametz**   10'

Poulenc
Gloria*   25'

interval

We Turned on the Light   c10'
BBC commission: first realisation

Bernstein
Chichester Psalms   18'

Susan Gritton *soprano**
Manickam Yogeswaran *singer*

The Shout
Orlando Gough *director*
National Youth Choir of Scotland
National Youth Choir of Great Britain
Rodolfus Choir
BBC Scottish Symphony Orchestra
Martyn Brabbins *conductor*

PROM 21 ⬅ ☐

7.30pm – c9.40pm

The Voice II
Wagner
The Mastersingers of Nuremberg –
Act 1 Prelude   11'

Michael Henry
Stand   c7'

Barber
Knoxville: Summer of 1915*   17'

We Turned on the Light   c10'
BBC commission: second realisation

interval

Prokofiev
Alexander Nevsky – cantata   40'

Christine Brewer *soprano**
Elena Manistina *mezzo-soprano*

The Shout
Orlando Gough *director*
BBC Symphony Chorus
Huddersfield Choral Society
BBC Symphony Orchestra
David Robertson *conductor*

Following the success of last year's all-day celebration of the violin, we turn this year's spotlight upon the most primal and direct medium of music-making – the human voice. Our day of song runs the gamut of vocal expression, from colourful sacred settings by Bernstein and Poulenc to Barber's nostalgic evocation of an all-American childhood and Wagner's tribute to a medieval German guild of Mastersingers, culminating in the massed choral outpourings of Prokofiev's patriotic cantata *Alexander Nevsky*. We also present the world premiere of a brand-new vocal work to a specially written text by Caryl Churchill on the threat of climate change, co-created by youth and adult choirs from across the UK working under the inspirational leadership of composer/choral director Orlando Gough and his off-the-wall vocal group The Shout, with 'rabble choirs' of volunteer singers recruited from Glasgow, London and the Prommers *(see right).*

🎵 **10.00am Come and Sing Workshop** (Holy Trinity Church, Prince Consort Road)
Just turn up and sing. See *Proms website* for details

Every Prom live on BBC Radio 3 and bbc.co.uk/proms • Advance Booking from 15 May • General Booking from 12 June: 020 7589 8212

70

FOCUS ON ... PROMS 20 & 21
THE VOICE

Orlando Gough introduces his choir The Shout and the new collaborative choral
work they will be helping to create for this year's Proms 'Voice' day

I started the choir The Shout in 1998 with Richard Chew, singer and composer. The singers are a wonderfully heterogeneous bunch, coming from diverse backgrounds – jazz, blues, gospel, contemporary classical, opera, rock 'n' roll, Indian classical ... In principle it's a mad idea. The usual Holy Grail of a choir – a blend of voices – is unattainable. But there are serious compensations.

Since its first ever project, an outdoor site-specific piece *The Shouting Fence*, about the Palestinians, The Shout has habitually worked with amateur singers. In 2001 we collaborated with the Belgian choreographer Alain Platel and 16 amateur choirs on *Because I Sing*, a kind of choral portrait of London, and were introduced to the joys of, amongst others, the London Gay Men's Chorus, Maspindzeli (the Georgian choir), Velvet Fist (the all-female socialist choir) and the Elmwood Singers (a group of friends from South-East London).

Since then we have collaborated with the wonderful Crouch End Festival Chorus, made contact with choirs from further away, such as Orfeon from Turkey, and made pieces with amateur singers in Bath, Amsterdam, Canterbury, Bexhill, Cardiff, Stuttgart ... working with every kind of choir as well as huge rabbles of singers who come together for one project and then dissolve into thin air.

I am constantly surprised and moved by the skill and commitment of amateur choirs. I love working with choirs with a very strong identity, like Velvet Fist, and choirs with no obvious identity at all, groups of singers whose only common ground is their love of singing. I'm intrigued by what these people do in their day jobs, I'm intrigued by their reasons for giving up their precious spare time to rehearse in bleak church halls and schoolrooms, and I'm intrigued by the possibility that a group of untrained singers can make a sublime noise.

Amo, amas, amat ... amateur.
It doesn't mean you're no good, it means you do it for love.

The new piece we'll be making for the Proms takes its inspiration from a mysterious, haunting, repetitive medieval poem, 'There was a man of double deed', which lists a catastrophic chain of consequences, ending eventually in death, that result from an apparently innocent action – 'sowed his garden full of seed'. With a new text by playwright Caryl Churchill, this form is applied to a contemporary issue of fierce importance – climate change – and becomes a kind of choral dance of death, playful but terrifying.

♪ **Join the Prommers' Rabble choir**
Always wanted to sing at the Proms? Why not join our Rabble Choir? Just check out the details on the Proms website and you too can take part in the world premiere performances of Caryl Churchill and Orlando Gough's new work, *We Turned on the Light*.

Every Prom live on BBC Radio 3 and bbc.co.uk/proms • Advance Booking from 15 May • General Booking from 12 June: 020 7589 8212

71

CONCERT LISTINGS

FOCUS ON ... PROM 24
HANDEL: ALEXANDER'S FEAST

Lindsay Kemp introduces Mozart's 'updating' of Handel

Weaned on the music of his older contemporaries rather than that of the then largely ignored composers of the previous generation, Mozart grew up with little or no knowledge of those two giants of the Baroque, Bach and Handel. When he did encounter their music in his mid-twenties, it left a mark on his own that never faded.

It was Baron van Swieten, a Viennese civil servant with antiquarian tastes, who introduced Mozart to this 'ancient' music. Van Swieten admired Handel's oratorios especially, and even arranged private performances of them; but, while he respected their essential qualities, he considered their orchestration thin and primitive by the standards of the 1780s. Mozart was asked to update them, and obliged by skilfully recasting four of the oratorios – including *Messiah* – for the kind of orchestra that he himself was familiar with, boosting Handel's basic Baroque line-ups with a Classical complement of flutes, clarinets and horns. The results are mellowing rather than garish, and bring a touch of middle-European warmth and serenity to Handel's sharp-edged, bracing scores.

But Mozart's intention was never that we should end up talking more about him than Handel, and indeed it is the latter's genius that should rightly be celebrated in these arrangements. In *Alexander's Feast*, written for St Cecilia's Day 1736 and depicting

the varied and profound effects of the music-making of the bard Timotheus on the assembled company at one of Alexander the Great's many victory parties, he produced a vivid work that seizes every opportunity to point up the poem's wide-ranging imagery. We get a moving evocation of the lonely death of Alexander's defeated foe, a thrilling call to arms, lugubrious music for a 'ghastly band' of dead Greeks; yet Handel also captures the poem's vein of humour, whether in a drinking scene or when showing us the great conqueror awakened by music to sensations of love. But then, he was one of the wisest and most humane of all musical dramatists – a title he can share with Mozart himself.

RIGHT
Handel playing the lyre: sculpture by Roubiliac, 1738

SUNDAY 30 JULY　　A

PROM 22　
6.30pm – c8.35pm

Haydn
Mass in B flat major, 'Heiligmesse'　40'

interval

Schubert
Symphony No. 9 in C major, 'Great'　52'

Lucy Crowe *soprano*
Alexandra Sherman *mezzo-soprano*
James Edwards *tenor*
Matthew Rose *bass*

BBC Singers
BBC Philharmonic
Gianandrea Noseda *conductor*

Haydn's life-affirming optimism in the first of his six 'late' Masses, written for the Princess Marie Hermenegild Esterházy, contrasts with Schubert's 'Great' final symphony, which, in Schumann's words, 'reveals to us something more than ... mere joy and sorrow ... It leads us into regions which – to our best recollection – we had never before explored.'

📷 **2.00pm Proms Film** (RGS)
Milos Forman's *Amadeus*. See page 120

MONDAY 31 JULY　　A

PROM 23
7.30pm – c9.35pm

Rimsky-Korsakov
The Maid of Pskov (Ivan the Terrible) – Overture　7'

Glazunov
Violin Concerto in A minor　21'

interval

Shostakovich
Symphony No. 8 in C minor　60'

Tasmin Little *violin*

BBC Philharmonic
Vassily Sinaisky *conductor*

Tasmin Little

Rimsky-Korsakov's opera tells of how Tsar Ivan the Terrible's discovery of a secret love-child led him to save a city from destruction. Written after his celebration of the Soviet people's heroism in his Seventh Symphony (see Prom 60), Shostakovich's searing Eighth presents a more tragic view of the human effects of war. In between Tasmin Little is the soloist in the lyrical concerto by Rimsky-Korsakov's friend and pupil, Glazunov *(below)*.

🎵 **1.00pm Proms Chamber Music**
See pages 110–13

Every Prom live on BBC Radio 3 and bbc.co.uk/proms • Advance Booking from 15 May • General Booking from 12 June: 020 7589 8212

72

PROM 24

7.00pm – c9.05pm

Handel, arr. Mozart
Alexander's Feast *(sung in German)*   88'

Sally Matthews *soprano*
Paul Agnew *tenor*
Roderick Williams *baritone*

Choir of The English Concert
The English Concert
Andrew Manze *conductor*

Handel's great oratorio, based on Dryden's ode to 'The Power of Music', presents the widest range of emotion within some of the composer's most operatic arias. While the minstrel Timotheus could 'raise a mortal to the skies', Handel, according to his librettist, could 'inspire life into the most senseless Words'. Andrew Manze, one of early music's most persuasive evangelists, conducts Mozart's rarely heard arrangement *(see panel, left)*.

Alexander the Great at the Battle of Issus: Roman mosaic

There will be one interval

🔲 **5.30pm Pre-Prom Talk** (RGS)
Discover *Alexander's Feast* with conductor Andrew Manze and Lindsay Kemp

PROM 25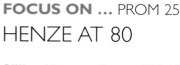

10.00pm – c11.35pm

Hans Werner Henze
Voices   90'

Mary King *mezzo-soprano*
Christopher Gillett *tenor*

London Sinfonietta
Oliver Knussen *conductor*

Oliver Knussen

Henze's vast song-cycle, a summation of his politically engaged earlier output, is the ideal work with which to mark his 80th birthday *(see panel, right)*. The diversity of languages and texts – including words by Bertolt Brecht *(below)*, who died 50 years ago – generates a corresponding range of styles and instrumentation, including Trinidadian steel drums and electric guitars.

There will be no interval

FOCUS ON ... PROM 25
HENZE AT 80

Gillian Moore offers an 80th-birthday tribute to the veteran German composer

Hans Werner Henze has spent the best part of his 80 years in diligent pursuit of beauty, in his life as much as in his art. The earthly paradise that he has created for himself in a villa among olive and lemon groves in the Roman Hills may, at first, appear at odds with a composer of politically engaged music that champions the cause of the poor, the oppressed and those ravaged by imperialist wars. But any talk with Henze very quickly turns to his continuing need to create an antidote to the spiritual and physical ugliness of a youth spent in small-town North Germany during the Third Reich.

Henze was a reluctant conscript in the Hitler Youth and later in the German army. His father, a Nazi sympathiser, once told the young Hans, still struggling with his sexuality, 'people like you belong in concentration camps'. Through all this, he took refuge in the world of ideas, in books and in music. A school friend stole the key for the cupboard of banned books in the local library, and the two boys devoured forbidden ideas in nightly raids. Mozart on the radio provided another ray of light, a first glimpse of 'a world of sun and pleasure ... My goal was Mozart, beauty, perfection, a new form of truth.'

Once the war was over, Henze set about creating his own musical world of beauty and truth at a frenzied pace that has barely slowed in the past 60 years. Ten symphonies, some 20 music-theatre works, a dozen or so ballet scores and numerous vocal and instrumental pieces have become established repertoire around the world. His recent orchestral work, *Five Messages for the Queen of Sheba* (Prom 60), is an orchestral suite from what he has said will be his last opera, *L'Upupa*, premiered at the 2003 Salzburg Festival *(pictured below)*.

'My interest in people and their voices is the principal matter in my whole work,' he has said. In his 1973 song-cycle *Voices*, Henze provides a compendium of different genres of song to give voice to the voiceless, to protest against injustice: a simple re-creation of an Italian folk song laments the death of a young resistance fighter at the hands of the Nazis; an acerbic Kurt Weill parody mocks American hypocrisy in Vietnam; a dark version of a barber-shop choir describes the lonely death of a factory worker. Yet Henze can't resist giving the last word to beauty, and the final song describes a Mayan festival of flowers.

LEFT
The 2003 Salzburg Festival premiere of *L'Upupa*

Every Prom live on BBC Radio 3 and bbc.co.uk/proms • Advance Booking from 15 May • General Booking from 12 June: 020 7589 8212

73

ELGAR/PAYNE: 'POMP AND CIRCUMSTANCE' MARCH NO. 6

A decade after he gave the world a new Elgar symphony to listen to, Anthony Payne has done it again and added a sixth 'Pomp and Circumstance' March to the canonic five. **Malcolm Hayes** tells the story

Anthony Payne's performing version of Elgar's Third Symphony – a masterly 'elaboration' of the sketches left by Elgar when he died – was one of English music's great success stories of the 1990s. So it might seem too good to be true that there's more where it came from. But there is. Elgar's five *Pomp and Circumstance* Marches – including of course No. 1, the time-honoured cornerstone of the Last Night of the Proms – now have a new sibling in the shape of No. 6, as once again brought to life by Payne. And for good measure, the new work's world premiere takes place on the exact date of Payne's 70th birthday.

Elgar's way of evolving a musical work or movement presents a serious challenge to anyone looking to generate a completed version from his unfinished sketches. These consist of isolated ideas only, with little obvious sense of how they were to develop, and next to none as to how Elgar might have assembled them into a final shape. In August 1997 *Musical Times* published an article by Elgar expert Christopher Kent, illustrating some material for a 'P & C 6' which had turned up among some papers in the library of the Royal School of Church Music.

Dating probably from the early 1930s, the sketches included an obvious main tune and other promising ideas (over one of which Elgar had written 'Jolly good'). They also appeared to complement another, near-indecipherable manuscript fragment already in the British Library – 'more an *aide-mémoire* than a sketch', says Payne, though he was able to deploy his in-depth knowledge of Elgar's style to draw on this also. As with the Third Symphony, he says, 'the same thing obtains: it's Elgar's material, and my working-out.'

The splendid main tune needed only 'tiny changes' as Payne extended its sequence of verses, whereas the March's rousing introduction and grand final flourish demanded much more creativity on his part. Having done his homework, his approach to making his performing version was rightly that of the composer rather than the academic. 'You just have to take your heart in your hands and do what's good.'

For Sir Andrew Davis, who will conduct the work's world premiere, as he did that of the Elgar/Payne Third Symphony back in 1998, it represents 'a fascinating new discovery … It's quite different in many ways from the other *Pomp and Circumstance* Marches, but it does remind me of the Third Symphony, in that it has the slightly more sombre, wistful quality of the music he was writing late on in his life rather than that characteristic sense of "robust health" you find in the music from his middle years.'

RIGHT
Elgar at work on his
Third Symphony in 1933

ABOVE LEFT
Anthony Payne, his
posthumous collaborator

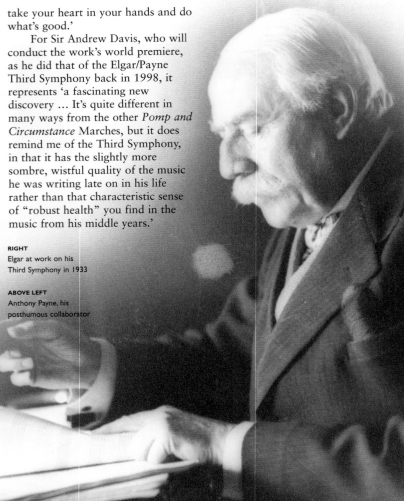

PROM 26

7.30pm – c9.40pm

Prokofiev
Symphony No. 1 in D major, 'Classical' *15'*

Britten
Les illuminations *25'*

interval

Elgar/Payne
Pomp and Circumstance March No. 6
in G minor *9'*
world premiere

J. S. Bach, orch. Andrew Davis
Passacaglia and Fugue in C minor,
BWV 582 *11'*

Shostakovich
Concerto for Piano, Trumpet and Strings
(Piano Concerto No. 1) *22'*

Nicole Cabell *soprano*
Evgeny Kissin *piano*
Sergei Nakariakov *trumpet*

BBC Symphony Orchestra
Sir Andrew Davis *conductor*

Nicole Cabell

Evgeny Kissin returns for Shostakovich's playful First Piano Concerto, partnered by fellow Russian virtuoso Sergei Nakariakov. The 2005 Cardiff Singer of the World makes her Proms debut in Britten's precocious settings of Rimbaud's dazzling prose-poems. And the latest fruit of Anthony Payne's historic collaboration with Elgar receives its world premiere on the younger partner's exact 70th birthday *(see panel, left)*, alongside a recent Bach orchestration by tonight's conductor.

PROM 27

7.00pm – c9.00pm

Toshio Hosokawa
Circulating Ocean *21'*
UK premiere

Mahler
Lieder eines fahrenden Gesellen *17'*

interval

Shostakovich
Symphony No. 15 in A major *45'*

Christopher Maltman *baritone*

BBC National Orchestra of Wales
Kazushi Ono *conductor*

Christopher Maltman

Tokyo-born Kazushi Ono, Music Director of La Monnaie in Brussels, conducts the UK premiere of Toshio Hosokawa's *Circulating Ocean*, premiered by Valery Gergiev at last year's Salzburg Festival *(see panel, right)*. Nature provides consolation in Mahler's autobiographical set of wayfaring songs, composed at the tender age of 23 following a painful break-up; while Mahler is one of the composers enigmatically quoted (alongside Rossini, Glinka and Wagner) in Shostakovich's death-haunted final symphony.

♪ **5.00pm Composer Portrait** (RAH)
Toshio Hosokawa. *See panel, right*

FOCUS ON … PROM 27
TOSHIO HOSOKAWA

As his music makes its Proms debut, the Japanese composer explains why he has long been obsessed by the sounds of the sea

Born in Hiroshima in 1955, a decade after the Americans dropped the A-bomb, Toshio Hosokawa initially studied piano and composition in Tokyo before continuing his studies in Germany, first with Isang Yun in West Berlin, then with Klaus Huber and Brian Ferneyhough in Freiburg. Since 1990 he himself has lectured at the famous New Music Summer Schools in Darmstadt, where he first had his own music performed in 1980, launching his international career.

Circulating Ocean, his first work to be heard at the Proms, was premiered at last year's Salzburg Festival, conducted by Valery Gergiev, alongside Russian tone-poems by Rakhmaninov and Rimsky-Korsakov.

Proms Composer Portrait
RAH, 5.00pm (before Prom 27)

Prior to the first Proms hearing of his orchestral music, Toshio Hosokawa talks to Andrew McGregor about his work and influences, and introduces the UK premieres of two contrasting chamber pieces: *Renka I* for mezzo-soprano and guitar (1986) and *Vertical Time Study I* for clarinet, piano and cello (1992).
See 'New Music', pages 44–8

But, though his music unites elements of both East and West, Hosokawa is no programmatic pictorialist. 'When I begin to compose,' he has written, 'I want there to be a deep connection at a basic level between myself and the sounds I create. I start listening to the sounds asleep in the depths of my body and I want to give them expression.' The sounds of the sea clearly run deep in his psyche. 'The resonating sounds of the sea,' he has written, 'are the sounds I heard while still in my mother's womb: the sound flowing through my mother's veins, the rhythmic beating of her distant heart … Perhaps these are the sounds the human species has continually heard throughout its long history, in the distant memory of its beginnings.'

These are again the sounds that roll, in powerful wave after wave, through *Circulating Ocean*. 'At first sight,' the composer concedes, 'the work might seem like a musical illustration of the eternal cycle of water, which rises as vapour from the sea, forms into clouds and falls again as rain upon the earth.' But the work is no simple science lesson, rather 'a metaphor for the human life-cycle. Born from a vast, limitless being, we ascend toward the heights, eventually begin our descent, experience violent storms and return again to an ocean of deep silence.'

Every Prom live on BBC Radio 3 and bbc.co.uk/proms • Advance Booking from 15 May • General Booking from 12 June: 020 7589 8212

75

KAROL SZYMANOWSKI

Symphony or concerto? **Adrian Jack** ponders the hybrid nature of the Polish composer's ambiguously titled work

Towards the end of his life, Karol Szymanowski turned away from the luxuriant and complex style of works like his First Violin Concerto (to be heard in Prom 65), Third Symphony ('The Song of the Night') and the opera *King Roger*, and developed a leaner, more 'neo-Classical' manner. There are parallels in his career with his contemporary, Bartók, and the solo piano writing in Szymanowski's *Symphonie concertante* (Symphony No. 4) predicts that of Bartók's Third Piano Concerto (Prom 44), with the hands often doubling each other in parallel as they outline highly ornamental melodies. By the time he wrote the work in 1932, Szymanowski was in need of an income to replace what he'd lost when forced to resign as rector of the Warsaw Academy of Music, and he started giving concert tours, taking the solo part in the first performance of the *Symphonie concertante* in Poznań (and later also in Brussels, Paris and London), although he dedicated the score, in hope, to his friend and compatriot, the famous pianist Arthur Rubinstein.

The *Symphonie concertante* is in three concise movements that last altogether about 25 minutes. While there are some passages of suspense leading to powerful climaxes, Szymanowski doesn't waste time with protracted endings. The first movement is both lyrical and capricious, with many switches of tempo and mood, and it includes a fully composed cadenza. In the gently atmospheric middle movement two orchestral soloists, a flute and a violin, are featured as well as the piano. The final movement is the most folk-like of the three, and is dominated by dance-like rhythms in lively triple time, culminating in a Dionysian whirl.

The question remains: is it a concerto or a symphony? The answer might be something like a symphonic concerto in which the element of solo display is restrained, although not altogether absent.

PROM 28

7.00pm – c9.10pm

Ravel
Mother Goose – Suite   17'

Szymanowski
Symphonie concertante
(Symphony No. 4)   25'

interval

Berlioz
Symphonie fantastique   50'

Piotr Anderszewski *piano*

Royal Scottish National Orchestra
Stéphane Denève *conductor*

Piotr Anderszewski

Ravel's magical suite of children's fairy-tales contrasts with the heady autobiographical dream-to-nightmare sequence of Berlioz's *Symphonie fantastique*, induced by his feverish love for the Irish actress Harriet Smithson *(below)*. Polish virtuoso Piotr Anderszewski joins the RSNO and its new French-born Music Director Stéphane Denève for his compatriot Karol Szymanowski's concerto-cum-symphony, written for the ailing composer's final European tour *(see panel, left)*.

PROM 29

10.15pm – c11.45pm

Cheikha Rimitti
Radio Tarifa

Given in association with the Festival of Muslim Cultures, this late-night Prom showcases music from both sides of the Strait of Gibraltar *(see panel, right)*. Cheikha Rimitti is the first lady of rai – the rebellious western Algerian popular song that speaks of the everyday struggles of the working people. Its direct, uninhibited lyrics have caused it to be banned on occasions since Algeria won its independence in 1962. With its fertile mix of styles, drawing together Iberian, Moorish, Yiddish, North African and Middle Eastern musics, from the past and present, into one uniquely adventurous melting-pot, Spain's Radio Tarifa should bring this concert to a roaring climax.

Cheikha Rimitti

There will be no interval

Every Prom live on BBC Radio 3 and bbc.co.uk/proms • Advance Booking from 15 May • General Booking from 12 June: 020 7589 8212

76

PROM 30

7.00pm – c9.00pm

Stravinsky
Symphony in Three Movements   23'

Janáček
Taras Bulba   25'

interval

Sibelius
Pohjola's Daughter   14'
Symphony No. 7 in C major   23'

**National Youth Orchestra
of Great Britain
Sir Colin Davis** conductor

Sir Colin Davis

Sir Colin Davis, one of today's greatest Sibelius interpreters, conducts the Finnish composer's *Kalevala*-inspired tone-poem and the single-movement symphony he wrote before his 30-year silence. The ever-talented National Youth Orchestra shows its mettle in Stravinsky's *Symphony in Three Movements*, partly inspired by newsreel footage of WWII, and Janáček's tribute to a legendary Cossack freedom-fighter, written in 1918 while the independence of the composer's Moravian homeland was under threat.

Broadcast on BBC TWO

♪ **5.00pm Beyond the Stave** (RAH)
A live performance of new works from the National Youth Orchestra's summer creative course. Introduced by Gillian Moore, Artistic Director of the London Sinfonietta, and Lincoln Abbotts, BBC Proms Learning Consultant

FOCUS ON ... PROM 29
RADIO TARIFA & CHEIKHA RIMITTI

Peter Culshaw introduces our late-night pairing of Algerian song from the 'mother of rai' and Andalusian fusion from Spain's hottest musical export

Cheikha Rimitti and Radio Tarifa's adventurous musical and lyrical innovations have made them among the most acclaimed artists in world music among critics and audiences alike. Born in 1923 in a village in western Algeria, Rimitti is a living legend, known as *la mamie du raï* for the way she, more than anyone else, has developed this unique style of Algerian music. Rai is rebellious music – Rimitti, from her earliest recordings in the 1950s to her latest European hit *N'ta Goudami*, has pioneered provocative, delicious songs about alcoholic oblivion, emigration, forced marriages, carnal pleasure and the miseries of poverty in Algeria. While younger artists, often plundering her repertoire and style, mix rai with rock or electronic dance music, Rimitti's sound is rooted in older styles, some of which stretch back centuries. Her real name is Saadia ('joyful') but the name didn't seem to fit her – she lost her parents at an early age and her life has often been a struggle. 'Misfortune was my teacher,' she believes. Her adopted name comes from the French 'remettez' – an order for a barman to set up another drink. 'My name became Rimitti because of alcohol,' she says – 'it's a great name.'

Radio Tarifa was created at the end of the 1980s, and the group's first CD, *Rumba Argelina*, in 1993 immediately attracted wide attention with its striking combination of Arabic, Andalusian, medieval and Sephardic music, conjuring up a modern version of the old Moorish kingdom of Al-Andaluz, where Christians, Jews and Muslims long lived together in some kind of harmony. Further award-winning recordings have gone deeper into Spanish folklore, flamenco and Renaissance music to create a sound that is refreshingly modern yet aware of the cultural history of Spain. The group uses Mediterranean instruments such as the oboe-like *ney*, *darbuka* (drum) and Arabic lutes, mixing them with medieval instruments like the crumhorn as well as electric bass and guitar. The name Tarifa comes from the beach in southern Spain where immigrants from North Africa often land, usually illegally.

Proms Saturday Matinee
3.00pm Cadogan Hall

**Academy of Ancient Music
Richard Egarr** *harpsichord/director*

From Bach to Mozart
See pages 108–9

Every Prom live on BBC Radio 3 and bbc.co.uk/proms • Advance Booking from 15 May • General Booking from 12 June: 020 7589 8212

77

FOCUS ON ... PROM 32

JULIAN ANDERSON PREMIERE

The composer explains why he joined a choir in order to write his new celebration of the beauties of nature

Heaven is Shy of Earth is written for mezzo-soprano, large chorus and orchestra, and lasts about 35 minutes. Purely orchestral movements frame a setting of sections from the Latin Mass, together with other texts in Latin and English. It is not a religious piece, being more akin to Janáček's *Glagolitic Mass* or Martinů's *Field Mass*, and like them it is essentially an 'outdoor' work celebrating the natural world.

One of the toughest tasks for today's composers is that of writing idiomatically singable choral music which isn't just pap. With this in mind, and in order to learn more about choral music from the inside, last year I joined a choir (the London Philharmonic) which taught me an enormous amount about what works for a chorus and what does not. I have tried to keep all this in mind so that, even where tricky, the choral writing is, I hope, idiomatic.

I have had enormous good luck in the ideal conditions with which the Proms have provided me in terms of performers. The mezzo part was written especially for Angelika

Kirchschlager, whose versatility and depth of sound I have always admired. And I am thrilled to be working again with Sir Andrew Davis, who has such a vividly dramatic style of conducting and who premiered my first Proms commission, *The Stations of the Sun*, in 1998.

The title comes from a poem by Emily Dickinson *(left)*, set as part of the 'Sanctus'. In it she says that the beauties of nature are such that even heaven would be almost ashamed of itself by comparison. This ecstatic vision of nature as sacrosanct expresses precisely the celebratory spirit of my piece.

PROM 31

4.00pm – c5.25pm

Mozart
Fantasia in F minor for mechanical organ, K608   11'

Shostakovich
The Gadfly – Credo;
The Cathedral Service   7'

Glière
Fugue on a Russian Christmas Song   2'

Glazunov
Fantasy, Op. 110   17'

Böhm
Chorale Prelude on 'Vater unser im Himmelreich'   4'

J. S. Bach
Chorale Prelude on 'Dies sind die heil'gen zehn Gebot', BWV 678   5'

Liszt
Fantasia and Fugue on 'Ad nos, ad salutarem undam'   28'

David Goode *organ*

Leading British organist David Goode puts the Royal Albert Hall's recently restored 'Father' Willis through its paces, taking in both of this year's major composer anniversaries, plus those of Glière (died 1956) and Glazunov (died 1936). Liszt's magnificent *Fantasia and Fugue* on a theme from Meyerbeer's opera *Le prophète*, written for Bach's centenary year, is prefaced by chorale preludes by Bach himself and Georg Böhm, whose music was an early influence on Bach's style.

There will be no interval

PROM 32

7.30pm – c9.40pm

Julian Anderson
Heaven is Shy of Earth   c35'
BBC commission: world premiere

interval

Ravel
Daphnis and Chloë   65'

Angelika Kirchschlager *mezzo-soprano*

BBC Symphony Chorus
BBC Symphony Orchestra
Sir Andrew Davis *conductor*

Angelika Kirchschlager

Julian Anderson's new Proms commission *(see panel, left)* is inspired by the poetry of Emily Dickinson, born in Massachusetts, where Anderson is now Harvard University's Professor of Music. Ravel's idyllic evocation of 'the Greece of my dreams' created a distinctly French work for Diaghilev's legendary Ballets Russes.

💬 **5.30pm Pre-Prom Talk** (RGS)
Julian Anderson introduces his new work in conversation with Ivan Hewett

---

Every Prom live on BBC Radio 3 and bbc.co.uk/proms • Advance Booking from 15 May • General Booking from 12 June: 020 7589 8212

78

PROM 33

7.30pm – c9.45pm

M. Haydn
Requiem   41'

interval

Mozart
Symphony No. 31 in D major,
K297 'Paris'   18'

Mass in C major, K317 'Coronation'   28'

Carolyn Sampson soprano
Hilary Summers mezzo-soprano
James Gilchrist tenor
Peter Harvey bass

Choir of The King's Consort
The King's Consort
Robert King conductor

Robert King

A colleague of Leopold and Wolfgang
Amadeus Mozart at the Salzburg court,
Michael Haydn (died 1806) was a strong
influence on the younger Mozart, and
parallels can be heard between their
respective Requiems (see panel, right).
Continuing our celebration of Mozart's
250th anniversary, Robert King also
conducts the convention-defying 'Paris'
Symphony and the Mozart Mass that
Salieri conducted at the coronation
of the Emperor Leopold II in Prague.

♪ **1.00pm Proms Chamber Music**
See pages 110–13

🗩 **6.00pm Pre-Prom Talk** (RAH)
Robert King in conversation with soprano
and broadcaster Catherine Bott

PROM 34

7.30pm – c9.25pm

Ravel
Rapsodie espagnole   15'

Henri Dutilleux
Métaboles   16'

interval

Ravel
Shéhérazade   17'

Roussel
Symphony No. 3   25'

Dame Felicity Lott soprano

BBC Philharmonic
Yan Pascal Tortelier conductor

The BBC Philharmonic's Paris-born
Conductor Laureate Yan Pascal Tortelier
leads an all-French programme presenting
Ravel's dual fascination with the mysteries
of the East and the brilliant rhythms
and colours of Spain. Henri Dutilleux,
the elder statesman of contemporary
French music (90 this year), explores
musical transformation in his Métaboles,

Dame Felicity Lott

a classic from
the 1960s, while
Roussel's Third
is a landmark French
symphony of the
20th century, from
a composer who
once advocated
the founding of
a 'Society for
Musical Eroticism'.

🗩 **6.00pm Pre-Prom Talk** (RAH)
Author and broadcaster Roger Nichols
introduces tonight's work by anniversary
composer Henri Dutilleux

FOCUS ON … PROM 33
THE 'OTHER' HAYDN

Robert King introduces the Requiem
by 'Papa' Haydn's younger brother

'All connoisseurs of music know, and
have known for some time, that as a
composer of sacred music Michael
Haydn ranks amongst the finest of
any age or nation …'

E. T. A. Hoffmann's high
opinion of Michael Haydn, brother
of the more famous Joseph, was
widely held. And Mozart expressed
a similarly positive reaction to
a composer who not only shares
this anniversary year with him but
worked alongside him in the city
where he was born. But, whereas
Mozart left Salzburg and its court in
1781, frustrated at what he viewed
as its overly provincial nature,
Haydn was very happy there, not
least because his particular strength
lay in writing vocal music: Salzburg
was the perfect breeding ground for
such a talent.

The relationship between Haydn
and the young Mozart was always
friendly, and the two maintained
contact even after Mozart left for
Vienna. Though Haydn never
formally taught him, we know that
Mozart often studied Haydn's works
(indeed, manuscripts in Mozart's
hand believed to have been written
by the youthful
prodigy were
later proven to
be works by Haydn, copied out as
an exercise), and Mozart certainly
had the opportunity to experience
Haydn's works both in rehearsal
and performance.

One such occasion fell in 1771 –
a black year for Haydn. Not only
had his baby daughter died just a
few days before her first birthday,
but his beloved patron, Archbishop
Sigismund, died on 16 December.
Although Haydn's awesome Requiem
was officially written for Sigismund,
and completed only a fortnight later,
it surely also reflected the loss of his
daughter. Mozart certainly heard
the work in rehearsal – he may even
have taken part in the performance –
and such a retentive mind must have
remembered both the occasion and
the setting. Whether as conscious
homage or because the imprint of a
fine work was still firmly fixed in his
mind 20 years afterwards, Mozart's
later unfinished masterpiece (see
Prom 57) shows an intriguing series
of musical parallels with Michael
Haydn's stirring Requiem.

Every Prom live on BBC Radio 3 and bbc.co.uk/proms • Advance Booking from 15 May • General Booking from 12 June: 020 7589 8212

79

FOCUS ON ... PROMS 35 & 36
HARVEY AND DILLON PREMIERES

Lynne Walker introduces the two new works which Ilan Volkov and the BBC Scottish Symphony Orchestra are bringing to the Proms

As its recent premiere in Glasgow revealed, *... towards a pure land* – the opening item in the first of the BBC SSO's two Proms and the first fruit of Jonathan Harvey's new role as the orchestra's Composer in Association – is an innovative and often visionary orchestral meditation. According to Buddhist philosophy, the 'pure land' represents a 'state of mind beyond suffering' and on this rosy landscape a small string group, named the 'Ensemble of Eternal Sound', glows serenely at the centre of an orchestra that creates its own dynamic brand of brilliant, worldly activity.

'The technical demands are extreme,' admits James Dillon *(above)* about the solo part in his own new piano concerto *Andromeda*, a BBC commission being premiered in the second BBC SSO Prom. In Greek legend, Andromeda, the offspring of Cepheus and Cassiopeia (night and darkness), was chained to a rock, at the mercy of the surging sea, until she was rescued by Perseus. 'But,' says Dillon, 'the invocation of the Andromeda myth serves only as an allegory ... the experience of unfolding drama set against an unrealised staging.' The large percussion section, including lion's roar, air horn and a football referee's whistle, is not, he says, 'as colourful as it looks'. No petrifying sound to represent the Gorgon's head then? 'There are of course some "exotica" in the score,' he admits, 'but they are used very discreetly and always as components within the sound complex.'

The latest of Dillon's consistently intriguing and challenging works, the concerto is in 15 sections arranged as a series of waves, one section giving birth to the next. The relationship of soloist and orchestra is constantly changing – a pattern of orchestral ripples, tiny shifts of instrumental colour, across which 'the piano casts its endless musical nets ... spinning trails into galaxies of sound'.

Proms Composer Portrait
RAH, 5.30pm
(before Prom 35)

Before the London premiere of his recent orchestral work *... towards a pure land*, Jonathan Harvey talks to Andrew McGregor and introduces performances of other works from his large catalogue of chamber music, including the trio *The Riot*. **See 'New Music', pages 44–8**

PROM 35
7.30pm – c9.30pm

Jonathan Harvey
... towards a pure land | 17'
London premiere

Mozart
Piano Concerto No. 25
in C major, K503 | 33'

interval

Schumann
Symphony No. 3 in E flat major,
'Rhenish' | 32'

Stephen Kovacevich *piano*

BBC Scottish Symphony Orchestra
Ilan Volkov *conductor*

Ilan Volkov

Stephen Kovacevich performs Mozart's magisterial late Piano Concerto in C, written in Vienna in the same year as *The Marriage of Figaro*, while we continue our Schumann 150th-anniversary survey with the symphonic tribute he paid in 1850 to his new Rhineland home. Though written for the opening of the BBC SSO's impressive new Glasgow home, where it was premiered earlier this year, associate composer Jonathan Harvey's 'pure land' is a notional one, free from poverty, danger and social friction, boasting gardens 'filled with heavenly flowers' *(see panel, left)*.

🎵 **5.30pm Composer Portrait** (RAH)
Jonathan Harvey. *See panel, left*

PROM 36
7.00pm – c9.10pm

Sibelius
En saga | 19'

James Dillon
Andromeda | c30'
BBC commission: world premiere

interval

Stravinsky
The Firebird | 46'

Noriko Kawai *piano*

BBC Scottish Symphony Orchestra
Ilan Volkov *conductor*

Noriko Kawai

Ilan Volkov and his Scottish forces return for a challenging new concerto from Scottish composer James Dillon, whose Violin Concerto enjoyed a successful premiere here in 2000 *(see panel, left)*. Sibelius's 'Fairy Tale' vies in its vivid storytelling with Stravinsky's magical folk-tale ballet.

🗣 **5.30pm Pre-Prom Talk** (RGS)
James Dillon introduces his new piano concerto in conversation with author and musicologist Richard Steinitz

Every Prom live on BBC Radio 3 and bbc.co.uk/proms • Advance Booking from 15 May • General Booking from 12 June: 020 7589 8212

80

PROM 37

10.15pm – c11.45pm

Steve Reich

Clapping Music   5'

Nagoya Marimbas   5'

Music for Mallet Instruments, Voices and Organ   19'

Drumming   45'

Colin Currie • Richard Benjafield • Sam Walton • Joby Burgess • Antoine Bedewi • Adrian Spillett • Dave Jackson • Owen Gunnell • Andrew Cottee *percussion*
Rowland Sutherland *piccolo*
Synergy Vocals

Steve Reich

To celebrate the 70th anniversary of one of the founding fathers of American Minimalism, this late-night concert contrasts the varied colours of *Music for Mallet Instruments, Voices and Organ* with the more intimately hypnotic Japanese modes of *Nagoya Marimbas*, also taking in the 1970s classic *Clapping Music* and the breakthrough work *Drumming*, composed after the composer's studies in Ghana.

There will be no interval

PROM 38   [Wp]

7.30pm – c9.35pm

John Adams

My Father Knew Charles Ives   27'

The Wound-Dresser   20'

interval

Harmonielehre   42'

Eric Owens *bass*

BBC Symphony Orchestra
John Adams *conductor*

The eclectic, post-Minimal music of the BBC SO's Artist in Association John Adams has made a major impact in this country in recent years. Here he presides over three of his own works, ranging from the Minimalism-meets-Romanticism of the thrilling 1985 classic *Harmonielehre*, through the introspective Walt Whitman setting *The Wound-Dresser*, to the autobiographical sound-memories of the more recent *My Father Knew Charles Ives (see panel, right)*.

♪ **4.00pm BBC Proms/Guardian Young Composers Concert** (CH)
See panel, right

💬 **6.00pm Pre-Prom Talk** (RAH)
Composer-conductor John Adams in conversation with Radio 3's Fiona Talkington

---

ADAMS CONDUCTS ADAMS

Keith Potter on how the ex-Minimalist finds harmony in diversity

The American composer John Adams grew up in the 1950s in, as he puts it, 'a household where Benny Goodman and Mozart were not separated'. He played clarinet in the local marching band and community orchestra; later, he studied at Harvard University with the composer Leon Kirchner. The 'profound cognitive dissonance', as Adams himself describes it, between Kirchner's severe serialism and his own experiences – as 'a hippie in all but wearing beads' – of listening to John Coltrane and the Rolling Stones made determining his ultimate direction as a composer difficult. Nevertheless, there were other models around. One was his older compatriot, Charles Ives, who had dealt with his own 'profound cognitive dissonances' by cheerfully ignoring them and writing music that audibly quoted, sometimes simultaneously, both the repertoire of those marching bands in which Adams later played and Western classical music, especially Beethoven.

Adams's *My Father Knew Charles Ives* is a misnomer, at least in so far as Adams's own father never actually met Ives. But this work celebrates, in a delightfully apt 'cognitive consonance', both Ives's multiplicity and the open-mindedness of Adams's father who, a bit like Ives himself, was

a businessman with an unusually developed passion for music.

While *My Father Knew Charles Ives* draws on both the reveille and Beethoven, *Harmonielehre* references Arnold Schoenberg, that dissonance-inclined teacher of Adams's own teacher, Kirchner. The fact that it manages to do this in the context of the kind of pattern-making repetition that is normally known as Minimalism is perhaps strange, and typically 'Adamsian'.

No less strange, and no less typical, is that *The Wound-Dresser*, the third Adams work in this concert, pretty much rejects Minimalism entirely in its dark exploration of Walt Whitman's poem about nursing war casualties. Adams's setting is also a response to the death of his own father from Alzheimer's Disease, which brings this rather elegantly conceived programme full circle.

Every Prom live on BBC Radio 3 and bbc.co.uk/proms • Advance Booking from 15 May • General Booking from 12 June: 020 7589 8212

81

FOCUS ON ... PROM 40

V IS FOR VENGEROV, VIOLIN AND VERBIER

Fresh back from his sabbatical year-out learning to dance the tango, violin virtuoso **Maxim Vengerov** is delighted to be performing Mozart again with the brilliant young players of the Verbier Festival Orchestra

Having turned 30 in 2004, Maxim Vengerov had planned to reward himself by taking the whole of 2005 off. But, as he explains, 'My sabbatical year didn't quite turn out as I'd planned and, although I didn't play my usual 80 to 90 concerts, I still ended up playing about 40.' Luckily, he also found the time to learn to play the viola, to improvise jazz on an electric violin and to dance the tango – all of which new skills he required in order to be able to perform Benjamin Yusupov's specially commissioned new *Viola-Tango-Rock Concerto*, which he premiered to great acclaim in Hanover in May 2005 and hopes to record next year and tour to the UK the year after.

But for now, it's back to Mozart – 'a giant of his time,' says Vengerov, 'and of all times. Even nowadays he's the greatest example of musicianship ever known.' For him, the Mozart of the violin concertos 'stands before us as still very young, but his spirituality is already very developed. The challenge of this music is not so much the difficulty of playing so many notes, as of creating the right sound – not only for the solo violin, but for all the strings. We have to reach an incredible harmony with each other.'

Which is why he's so pleased to be playing with the young musicians of the Verbier Festival Orchestra. 'We met for the first time in Israel last year, spent two wonderful weeks in a kibbutz, played Mozart concerts in Tel Aviv and Jerusalem, and then began recording the music in February. It's been fascinating to see these young people growing before my eyes.'

SATURDAY 12 AUGUST — A

PROM 39 ⓦ

6.30pm – c8.45pm

Schnittke
(K)ein Sommernachtstraum — 11'

Mozart
Violin Concerto No. 5
in A major, K219 'Turkish' — 29'

interval

Shostakovich
Symphony No. 4 in C minor — 60'

Janine Jansen *violin*

European Union Youth Orchestra
Vladimir Ashkenazy *conductor*

Janine Jansen

Former Radio 3 New Generation Artist Janine Jansen returns after her thrilling First Night performance last year to celebrate the Mozart anniversary with his 'Turkish' violin concerto. We continue our Shostakovich centenary survey with the symphony that had to wait 25 years for its premiere after the composer felt forced to withdraw it in the wake of the notorious *Pravda* attack of 1936. And the concert begins with Alfred Schnittke's mischievous response to a request for a Shakespeare-related work.

Broadcast on BBC TWO

🎬 **2.00pm Proms Film** (RGS)
Tony Palmer's *Testimony.*
See page 120

SUNDAY 13 AUGUST — B

PROM 40 → ⓦ

4.00pm – c6.15pm

Mozart
Violin Concerto No. 1
in B flat major, K207 — 21'

Sinfonia concertante
in E flat major, K364 — 30'

interval

Violin Concerto No. 4
in D major, K218 — 22'

Symphony No. 29 in A major, K201 — 23'

Lawrence Power *viola*

UBS Verbier Festival Chamber Orchestra
Maxim Vengerov *violin/conductor*

Maxim Vengerov

Maxim Vengerov, the heir to Heifetz's bow, returns to play and direct an all-Mozart programme comprising two violin concertos, the collegial *Sinfonia concertante* (with brilliant British violist Lawrence Power) and the eloquent symphony that Mozart wrote aged only 18 (*see panel, left*).

Recorded for future broadcast on BBC ONE and BBC FOUR

Every Prom live on BBC Radio 3 and bbc.co.uk/proms • Advance Booking from 15 May • General Booking from 12 June: 020 7589 8212

82

PROM 41

8.00pm – c10.00pm

Steven Stucky
Second Concerto for Orchestra   26'
UK premiere

interval

Ravel
Piano Concerto in G major   22'

Musorgsky, orch. Ravel
Pictures at an Exhibition   30'

François-Frédéric Guy *piano*

Philharmonia Orchestra
Esa-Pekka Salonen *conductor*

Esa-Pekka Salonen rejoins his former
British orchestra for the UK premiere of
a new Pulitzer Prize-winning showpiece
he premiered with his American orchestra
in LA in 2004 *(see panel, right)*. Ravel's
sparkling Piano Concerto and Musorgsky's
vivid suite of sound-paintings, as retouched
by Ravel, complete the picture.

Esa-Pekka Salonen

*Second half recorded for future broadcast
on BBC FOUR*

🔲 **6.30pm Pre-Prom Talk** (RGS)
Steven Stucky introduces his *Second
Concerto for Orchestra* in conversation
with Adrian Thomas, Professor of Music
at Cardiff University

PROM 42

7.30pm – c9.20pm

Sibelius
The Oceanides   8'

R. Strauss
Four Last Songs   22'

interval

Bartók
Concerto for Orchestra   40'

Soile Isokoski *soprano*

Finnish Radio Symphony Orchestra
Sakari Oramo *conductor*

Sakari Oramo

Sakari Oramo returns,
to the Proms with his
new Finnish orchestra
and the only tone-poem
by Finnish composer,
Sibelius to be based
on Greek rather than
Nordic mythology.
Finnish soprano Soile
Isokoski *(below)* sings Strauss's valedictory
Four Last Songs (posthumously premiered
in the Royal Albert Hall in 1950) and we
mark Bartók's 125th anniversary with the
orchestral showpiece he composed while
dying in American exile.

♪ **1.00pm Proms Chamber Music**
See pages 110–13

FOCUS ON ... PROM 41
STEVEN STUCKY PREMIERE

**The LA Phil's charismatic Music Director brings
to the UK a new concerto tailor-made to suit
him and his American orchestra**

When André Previn invited him to
become composer-in-residence with
the Los Angeles Philharmonic back in
1988, Steven Stucky could hardly
have imagined his association would
last for nearly 20 years. Currently the
orchestra's Consulting Composer for
New Music, he works closely with
charismatic music director Esa-Pekka
Salonen, who conducted the premiere
of Stucky's *Second Concerto for
Orchestra* in 2004, during the
opening season of the LA Phil's
striking new Disney Concert Hall,
and who now brings it to the Proms
with the Philharmonia Orchestra, of
which he was Principal Guest
Conductor for almost a decade. And,
to emphasise their relationship,
Salonen's name is literally written into
the score, with the letters 'ESA' (the
German names for the notes E, E flat
and A) appearing as one of the
musical mottos in the first movement,
entitled 'Overture (with Friends)'.

As with Bartók's standard-bearing
Concerto for Orchestra from 1943 (to
be heard the following night, courtesy
of Salonen's fellow Finn, Sakari
Oramo), individual members of the
orchestra get their virtuoso turns, as
do entire sections. 'There's some very
bright music in the first and third
movements,' says Stucky, 'though the
slow second movement is
considerably darker in some ways.'

Stucky unashamedly asserts
a non-avant-garde perspective.
It's figures like Debussy, Stravinsky,
Bartók, Sibelius, Ravel and Berg to
whom he refers as his 'household
gods'. 'Boulez, Xenakis and Donatoni
have been important in my life, but
you don't hear it so easily in my
music. It's just that the music which
resonates with me the most is not the
most stridently modernist.'

The *Second Concerto for
Orchestra* shares its Prom with Ravel's
Piano Concerto, which receives a
recognisable homage in Stucky's first
movement, and with Ravel's skilful
orchestration of Musorgsky's *Pictures
at an Exhibition*. Stucky recognises
himself as 'coming at the end of the
train of which Musorgsky occupies
one of the leading cars'. Three gifted
20th-century orchestral colourists in
one Prom? 'It's almost like a family
snapshot,' agrees Stucky.

Every Prom live on BBC Radio 3 and bbc.co.uk/proms • Advance Booking from 15 May • General Booking from 12 June: 020 7589 8212

83

FOCUS ON ... PROM 45
LUTOSLAWSKI: PAROLES TISSÉES

Ian Bostridge on the amazing musical world that the Polish master wove from French surrealist texts for the tenor Peter Pears

Some English tenors walk in the shadow of Peter Pears, unable to escape the echo of his inimitable voice; others are happy to follow in his footsteps and to claim his repertoire as their own. Such a tenor is Ian Bostridge, who has already mastered much of the music that Benjamin Britten wrote for his partner, from the *Serenade* to *The Turn of the Screw*, and who is currently learning the role of Aschenbach for ENO's new production of *Death in Venice* next summer. But Britten, of course, wasn't the only composer who wrote pieces for Pears to sing. 'This year I'm doing two others,' says Bostridge: 'Henze's *Kammermusik 1958*,

in honour of the composer's 80th birthday, and Lutoslawski's *Paroles tissées*.' It's the latter work that we'll hear him sing at the Proms.

A diaphanously scored setting of four surrealist poems, or 'tapestries', by the French writer Jean-François Chabrun – not so much recounting as indirectly illuminating aspects of the medieval French tale of courtly love, *La Châtelaine de Vergy* – this richly allusive cycle of 'woven words' was premiered by Pears at the 1965 Aldeburgh Festival.

A famously word-sensitive and literate tenor – he was a post-doctoral fellow in History at Corpus Christi College, Oxford, before embarking on a full-time singing career – Bostridge has long wanted to tackle the work: 'I love poetry-as-music set to music. And in this case, where a French composer might have felt compelled to try to set the poems as meaning, Lutoslawski, being non-French, felt free to set them purely as sound. If there is a story behind the words, I haven't rationalised it. There's definitely a "journey", in so far as it starts tentatively, gets serious in the middle and then fizzles out – rather like life really! But I'm just amazed at how wonderful it is, what an incredible world it conjures up. I really hope to sing it a lot from now on!'

TUESDAY 15 AUGUST
PROM 43
7.30pm – c9.45pm

Schumann
Manfred – Overture — 12'

Beethoven
Violin Concerto in D major — 45'

interval

Mendelssohn
Symphony No. 3 in A minor, 'Scottish' — 39'

Christian Tetzlaff violin

BBC Symphony Orchestra
Jiří Bělohlávek conductor

Christian Tetzlaff

The 'dramatic poem' *Manfred* by Anglo-Scot Byron appealed to Schumann's Romantic sensibilities in the same way that Scotland's 'comfortless, inhospitable solitude' inspired Mendelssohn. By contrast, the lyricism of Beethoven's Violin Concerto rejects the generally 'heroic' struggles of his middle period, seemingly searching for nothing more, and nothing less, than beauty for its own sake.

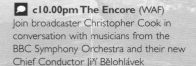
🔲 c10.00pm The Encore (WAF)
Join broadcaster Christopher Cook in conversation with musicians from the BBC Symphony Orchestra and their new Chief Conductor Jiří Bělohlávek

WEDNESDAY 16 AUGUST
PROM 44
7.30pm – c9.25pm

Dohnányi
Symphonic Minutes — 11'

Bartók
Piano Concerto No. 3 — 25'

interval

Stravinsky
The Rite of Spring — 33'

Garrick Ohlsson piano

Budapest Festival Orchestra
Iván Fischer conductor

Bartók's exhilarating Third Piano Concerto marks the welcome return of American pianist Garrick Ohlsson. Hungary's leading orchestra and conductor also perform a curtain-raising suite of miniatures by fellow Hungarian Ernő Dohnányi, grandfather of conductor Christoph von Dohnányi (see Prom 56), and Stravinsky's earthy, riot-provoking ballet depicting pagan Russian rites.

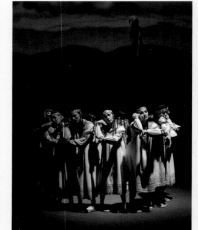

Every Prom live on BBC Radio 3 and bbc.co.uk/proms • Advance Booking from 15 May • General Booking from 12 June: 020 7589 8212

84

THURSDAY 17 AUGUST A

PROM 45 ➔

7.00pm – c9.05pm

Stravinsky
Dumbarton Oaks   15'

Lutoslawski
Paroles tissées   16'

Wagner
Siegfried Idyll   18'

interval

Mozart
Symphony No. 41 in C major,
K551 'Jupiter'   36'

Ian Bostridge *tenor*

Orchestra of St Luke's
Donald Runnicles *conductor*

Ian Bostridge

New York's Orchestra of St Luke's continues this year's Mozart survey under its Principal Conductor Donald Runnicles, a popular guest with the BBC SO. Stravinsky's Baroque-inflected *Dumbarton Oaks* and Lutoslawski's intricate 'Woven Words' *(see panel, left)* contrast with Wagner's lyrical *Siegfried Idyll*, based on themes from the third of his *Ring* operas (see Prom 3) and originally performed on Christmas morning 1870 in celebration of his wife Cosima's 33rd birthday and the birth of their first son.

THURSDAY 17 AUGUST E

PROM 46 ⬅

10.00pm – c11.30pm

Mozart
Rondo in A minor, K511   10'

Sonata in A major, K331   23'

Fantasia in D minor, K397   6'

Adagio in B minor, K540   10'

Rondo in D major, K485   6'

Sonata in A minor, K310   21'

András Schiff *piano*

Late-night Mozart, marking the composer's 250th anniversary in a rare Proms solo recital. András Schiff, a distinguished interpreter of the Classical piano repertoire, promises an intense and enthralling sequence of some of Mozart's finest keyboard works *(see panel, right)*.

András Schiff

There will be no interval

FOCUS ON ... PROM 46
SCHIFF PLAYS MOZART

András Schiff reveals how playing Mozart's own fortepiano has coloured his approach to performing the music on a modern grand

For some it's the symphonies, for others it's the operas, but pianist András Schiff is in no doubt: 'I would not put anything in Mozart's output higher than the piano concertos,' he says with conviction, having recorded the entire cycle with the Camerata Salzburg under the late Sándor Végh. 'Having said that, whenever you play anything by Mozart, you always hear the operas – every theme is like a character. And, if I had to choose just one of all the operas, it would always be *Cosi*' – of whose 'miraculous' qualities he speaks with conviction too, having conducted it himself at the Edinburgh Festival in 2001. 'After which, when I went back to the piano music, I saw it all in a new light.'

When it came to choosing the pieces for his late-night solo Prom – 'a really daring, maybe even crazy idea,' he admits, 'to put something so intimate as Mozart's piano music in so vast a venue' – he was of course spoilt for choice. But, as he says, 'even Mozart has his peaks and his lesser peaks – what I would call his "occasional" compositions. And so, in designing a programme, I've tried not only to select the pieces I love the most but to create what I call a "composition within tonalities", with a variety of longer and shorter pieces, some in rondo form, some in sonata form, and so on.'

Formally, this 'composition' is framed by the key of A minor. 'You can count on one hand the works Mozart wrote in this key,' says Schiff, 'and whenever he did, it always strikes a tragic nerve.' The 'extraordinary' A minor Rondo with which he'll begin is one of the works he recorded – back in the Mozart bicentenary year, 1991 – on Mozart's own fortepiano in the very room where the composer was born. 'I always bear in mind what the music sounded like on that instrument. You can't imitate it on a modern piano but something stuck in my soul.'

Every Prom live on BBC Radio 3 and bbc.co.uk/proms • Advance Booking from 15 May • General Booking from 12 June: 020 7589 8212

85

| FRIDAY 18 AUGUST **B** | SATURDAY 19 AUGUST **C** | SUNDAY 20 AUGUST **C** |

PROM 47

7.30pm – c9.55pm

PROM 48

6.30pm – c8.55pm

PROM 49

6.30pm – c9.55pm

Shostakovich
The Golden Age – excerpts   25'

Schnittke
Viola Concerto   34'

interval

Tchaikovsky
Symphony No. 6 in B minor,
'Pathétique'   48'

Yuri Bashmet *viola*

London Symphony Orchestra
Valery Gergiev *conductor*

Yuri Bashmet

Valery Gergiev's all-Russian Prom continues the Shostakovich centenary theme with excerpts from the composer's politically correct, anti-Capitalist ballet *The Golden* Age. Schnittke's bracing, humorous Viola Concerto was written for tonight's soloist, whose name is encoded into its music. While Schnittke later saw its last movement as a 'slow and sad overview of life on the threshold of death', Tchaikovsky poured equal passion into his final symphony, before giving up his struggle with life within 10 days of its premiere.

Lyadov
From the Apocalypse   9'

Sibelius
Violin Concerto in D minor   33'

interval

Shostakovich
Symphony No. 13 in B flat minor,
'Babi Yar'   60'

Bass soloist of the Mariinsky Theatre
Vadim Repin *violin*

**Chorus and Orchestra of the
Mariinsky Theatre (Kirov Opera)**
Valery Gergiev *conductor*

Vadim Repin

The second of three Shostakovich-anniversary concerts conducted by Valery Gergiev brings the composer's harrowing choral symphony inspired by the Nazi-led massacre of Jews at Babi Yar in September 1941 – a work which implicitly also questioned the ethics of the Soviet state. One of Russia's leading violinists performs one of the greatest concertos of the Romantic era, written at a time when its composer's native land was still under tsarist Russian rule.

Broadcast on BBC TWO

Shostakovich
Lady Macbeth of the Mtsensk District *(concert performance; sung in Russian)*   160'

Soloists, Chorus and Orchestra of the Mariinsky Theatre (Kirov Opera)
Valery Gergiev *conductor*

Valery Gergiev

As the high point of our Shostakovich centenary exploration Valery Gergiev brings his Mariinsky Theatre forces from St Petersburg for a complete concert performance of the composer's second (and last completed) opera – a work, at once murderously funny and bleakly tragic, whose initial success led to three different stagings running simultaneously in Moscow before Stalin came to see it and effectively had it banned *(see panel, right)*.

There will be one interval

2.00pm Proms Film (RGS)
Grigori Kozintsev's *Hamlet* (music by Shostakovich). See *page 120*

5.00pm Pre-Prom Talk (RGS)
An introduction to *Lady Macbeth* by Marina Frolova-Walker

Every Prom live on BBC Radio 3 and bbc.co.uk/proms • Advance Booking from 15 May • General Booking from 12 June: 020 7589 8212

FOCUS ON ... PROM 49

SHOSTAKOVICH: LADY MACBETH OF THE MTSENSK DISTRICT

Andrew Huth on the opera whose all-out assault on audience sensibilities provoked an all-out attack from the Soviet state

The opera *Lady Macbeth of the Mtsensk District* was completed in 1932, when Shostakovich was still only in his late twenties, and is the climax of his amazingly prolific early period when music poured out of him, often chaotic and disorganised, frequently wildly satirical, much of it intended for theatre, film or ballet. With its huge cast and variety of situations, *Lady Macbeth* allowed full scope to all these aspects.

The subject was freely adapted from a 19th-century story by Nikolay Leskov, but the treatment is very 20th-century. Katerina, the Lady Macbeth of the title, is the neglected wife of a feeble provincial merchant dominated by his brutal father. Katerina arranges their murders to make way in her bed for the handsome young workman Sergey. Katerina alone achieves some kind of dignity and even redemption through her passion for the unworthy Sergey. Most of the other characters are brutalised and mocked in music that ranges from the farcical to the terrifying, from the pathetically human to the appallingly inhuman. In *Lady Macbeth* Shostakovich mustered every shock tactic at his disposal to launch an all-out assault on the audience's sensibilities and create a music-drama of enormous but ambiguous power.

One person who didn't like it was Stalin. He walked out of a performance in Moscow in December 1935, and a few days later there appeared the notorious article in *Pravda* entitled 'Chaos instead of Music'. This was a signal that from now on Soviet composers would have to toe the party line and provide healthy, uplifting music for the masses. Shostakovich withdrew his enormous Fourth Symphony, and with the Fifth made a successful bid for rehabilitation. Within a few years, his Seventh (the 'Leningrad') would become a symbol of Russia's wartime resistance to Hitler, and in works from the 1950s and 1960s we can hear him treading a delicate path between personal expression and orthodox Soviet idioms. The late works seem to withdraw into a private world of bleakness and anguish, redeemed by rare but deeply moving moments of tenderness.

Lady Macbeth was revived in 1961, with some of its more 'offensive' features removed, and with the new title *Katerina Ismailova*. In the same year the Fourth Symphony was finally performed in public. Shostakovich's evident happiness at hearing these works again after 25 years was nevertheless tinged with bitterness. 'You ask if I would have been different without "Party Guidance"? Yes, almost certainly. No doubt the line that I was pursuing when I wrote the Fourth Symphony would have been stronger and sharper in my work. I would have displayed more brilliance, used more sarcasm, I could have revealed my ideas openly instead of having to resort to camouflage ...'

ABOVE LEFT
Shostakovich, c1930, at the time he began his opera

BELOW & RIGHT
Lady Macbeth of the Mtsensk District: scenes from the 1934 Leningrad premiere of the opera (*below*) and Roman Balayan's 1989 film of Leskov's original story

Every Prom live on BBC Radio 3 and bbc.co.uk/proms • Advance Booking from 15 May • General Booking from 12 June: 020 7589 8212

87

GRUBER CONDUCTS GRUBER

Annette Morreau meets a former Vienna choirboy turned demonic chansonnier with a hidden agenda to keep music free of 'plinky-plonky'

'*Franky*? It's my bestseller!' declares jovial Austrian composer, HK ('Nali') Gruber. Nali (a nickname he earned as a lad in the Vienna Boys' Choir) wrote *Frankenstein!!* – subtitled 'A pan-demonium for chansonnier and orchestra' – in 1976. Simon Rattle conducted the tumultuous premiere in Liverpool, with Nali himself as the chansonnier, since when it has been performed over 1,500 times – indeed Gruber holds the record as the most performed Austrian composer alive.

There are not many orchestral scores that instruct the performers to 'keep poker-faced! No laughing, no grinning!' or that demand of the soloist that he/she also plays siren, kazoo, soprano melodica and two swanee whistles! But then, there are not many composers who have such a wicked sense of humour, digging away at the school of 'plinky-plonky' and 'hard-core' ensembles with ineffable good will. 'In Austria,' says Gruber, 'I'm not known as a "modern" composer, because I write in C major. It's like giving garlic to a vampire!' And vampires, John Wayne, Mister Superman, Batman and Robin, and all sorts of rats, bats and 'monsterlets' figure in the surreal children's rhymes by H. C. Artmann that make up the text of Gruber's 'pan-demonium'. 'The consonants should explode like bombs,' he says – as indeed they do whenever Nali himself appears as chansonnier extraordinaire.

Hidden Agenda, his newest work (due to be premiered in Lucerne just before it comes to the Proms), is exactly that: a riddle based on a tone-row. 'I always use rows,' Gruber explains, 'but the consequences are Nali, not Schoenberg.' Or, to de-code, not the school of 'plinky-plonky'. But this is a borrowed row 'full of tonal and chromatic possibilities' that allow for simultaneous inversions and transpositions. With half the piece still to be written, 'I don't know where I'll land,' he laughs.

PROM 50

7.30pm – c9.45pm

Berlioz
Overture 'Les francs-juges' 12'

James MacMillan
The Confession of Isobel Gowdie 25'

interval

Elgar
Symphony No. 2 in E flat major 60'

London Symphony Orchestra
Sir Colin Davis *conductor*

Sir Colin Davis, who celebrates his 80th birthday next year, conducts his twin passions of Elgar and Berlioz. While a moonlit cavern is the meeting place for the secret tribunal of Berlioz's *francs-juges*, the witch-hunts of the Scottish Reformation inspired James MacMillan's *Confession of Isobel Gowdie*, which launched his international career at its Proms premiere in 1990.

James MacMillan

Broadcast on BBC FOUR

♪ **1.00pm Proms Chamber Music**
See pages 110–13

💬 **6.00pm Pre-Prom Talk** (RAH)
James MacMillan introduces *The Confession of Isobel Gowdie* in conversation with Radio 3's Stephanie Hughes

---

PROM 51

7.00pm – c8.50pm

R. Strauss
Don Juan 17'

Chausson
Poème de l'amour et de la mer 27'

interval

Shostakovich
Symphony No. 6 in B minor 30'

Susan Graham *mezzo-soprano*

Gustav Mahler Jugendorchester
Philippe Jordan *conductor*

Susan Graham

The pan-European Mahler Youth Orchestra makes a welcome return under a young Swiss conductor making his Proms debut. Strauss's early tone-poem explores the amorous conquests of the legendary Don Juan. American mezzo Susan Graham makes her Proms debut in Chausson's lilac-scented seaside romance. And the concert closes with the symphony that Shostakovich claimed was written to convey 'the mood of spring, joy and life' – a politically cautious comment that hides a deeper ambivalence.

Broadcast on BBC FOUR

Every Prom live on BBC Radio 3 and bbc.co.uk/proms • Advance Booking from 15 May • General Booking from 12 June: 020 7589 8212

PROM 52 ⬅

10.00pm – c11.20pm

HK Gruber
Hidden Agenda   c10'
UK premiere

Weill
Kiddush   4'

Eisler
Liturgie vom Hauch, Op. 21 No. 1   6'

Weill
Berlin Requiem – 'Zu Potsdam unter
den Eichen'   3'

Eisler
Über das Töten, Op. 21 No. 2   2'

Weill
Berlin Requiem – 'Legende vom toten
Soldaten'   4'

Eisler
Ferner Streiken: 50,000 Holzarbeiter,
Op. 19 No. 1   2'

HK Gruber
Frankenstein!!   30'

Daniel Hyde organ

BBC Singers
BBC Symphony Orchestra
HK Gruber conductor/chansonnier

HK Gruber is the chansonnier in his own
irreverent 1970s 'pan-demonium', famously
premiered and championed by Simon
Rattle, and conducts his latest work fresh
from its premiere at the Lucerne Festival
(see panel, left). Choral works by Weill and
Eisler mark the 50th anniversary of the
death of their close collaborator, Bertolt
Brecht.

There will be no interval

PROM 53

7.30pm – c9.40pm

Mark-Anthony Turnage
A Relic of Memory   17'
UK premiere

Prokofiev
Piano Concerto No. 2 in G minor   34'

interval

Rakhmaninov
The Bells   38'

Nikolai Lugansky piano
Tatiana Monogarova soprano
Vsevolod Grivnov tenor
Sergei Leiferkus baritone

London Philharmonic Choir
Philharmonia Chorus
London Philharmonic Orchestra
Vladimir Jurowski conductor

Vladimir Jurowski

The LPO and its
dynamic Principal
Guest Conductor
Vladimir Jurowski
preface a Russian
pairing of Prokofiev's
virtuosic Second
Piano Concerto and
Rakhmaninov's birth-to-death symphony
with the UK premiere of Mark-Anthony
Turnage's equally bell-toned musical
memento mori (see panel, right).

Broadcast on BBC FOUR

🗨 **6.00pm Pre-Prom Talk** (RAH)
Mark-Anthony Turnage introduces
A Relic of Memory in conversation
with Rob Cowan

FOCUS ON ... PROM 53
MARK-ANTHONY TURNAGE PREMIERE

Anthony Burton gives ringing endorsement to a new work
in which musical memories chime with thoughts of mortality

Mark-Anthony
Turnage has
always been a
collaborative
composer,
working closely
with jazz soloists,
preferring to write chamber music
for musicians he knows well, and
structuring his career around a series
of associations that have allowed him
to develop pieces under workshop
conditions: with the City of
Birmingham Symphony Orchestra,
with English National Opera, with
the BBC Symphony Orchestra, and
now as Composer in Residence with
the London Philharmonic Orchestra.
This is the orchestra that gives his *A
Relic of Memory* its UK premiere at
the Proms, with its own Choir and
its Principal Guest Conductor
Vladimir Jurowski. But the work
itself bears witness to Turnage's
continuing links to another
conductor who appears later this
season, having been workshopped in
Berlin and first performed there in
October 2004 under the direction of
Sir Simon Rattle.

Named after a poem by Seamus
Heaney, *A Relic of Memory* is a kind
of memorial frieze, setting a few
lines of a death-haunted Shakespeare
sonnet and phrases from the Requiem
Mass with obsessive intensity. At its

conclusion, it incorporates almost
unaltered Turnage's *Calmo*, a hushed
choral elegy for his friend Sue Knussen
that was first heard at the Proms
in 2004. The element of memory
is invoked musically by the work's
derivation from the opening of Bach's
St Matthew Passion, which the
composer says is 'there in almost
every bar', its intervals 'stretched to
breaking-point'. And the piece should
make an unexpectedly appropriate
companion for Rakhmaninov's
choral symphony *The Bells*, through
its own use of bell sounds: hand
bells, desk bells, tuned gongs and a
tumultuous full-orchestra jangling to
accompany Shakespeare's lines:
   ... hear the surly sullen bell
   Give warning to the world
       that I am fled.

Every Prom live on BBC Radio 3 and bbc.co.uk/proms • Advance Booking from 15 May • General Booking from 12 June: 020 7589 8212

89

OSVALDO GOLIJOV

Michael Church on the Argentine composer's eclectic musical roots

Born into a Russian-Romanian-Jewish family in La Plata, Argentina, Osvaldo Golijov's earliest memories are of sitting under his mother's piano, which she also taught him to play. 'I was never much into practising,' he admits, 'but I was very curious about how things were put together. How Bach, for example, could write three or four melodies that fitted together.' He started composing as a child, but the impetus for his creative career came when Astor Piazzolla came to town.

'Piazzolla was the man who made me believe that it was possible for me to create, that music was not something that had to be imported from Europe.' La Plata's Jewish community was largely assimilated but, when General Videla came to power, everything changed. 'Under a government with Nazi roots, I knew that you could never be openly Jewish and proud of it.' His response was to move to Jerusalem, where he absorbed the rich mix of influences that were to find their fullest expression in his song-cycle *Ayre*, with its blend of Christian, Islamic and Jewish elements.

He went on to study in the USA with George Crumb and Oliver Knussen, and began to work with the Kronos Quartet, who in turn introduced him to the Romanian gypsy band Taraf de Haïdouks, thus broadening his already eclectic range. The *Pasión según San Marcos* ('St Mark Passion') which Helmuth Rilling invited him to compose for the Millennium put him on the international map; its intermittently raw vocal style, samba rhythms and Bahian drumming signalled a triumphant assertion that this hitherto quintessentially European musical form could grow in very different soil.

Its most beautiful number, 'Lúa descolorida' ('Colourless Moon') – later reorchestrated as the centrepiece of the *Three Songs* – was originally composed for the soprano Dawn Upshaw, who gives the *Songs* their UK premiere in Prom 54. Golijov says he 'saw a rainbow' when he first realised the range of colour in her voice. She returns the compliment: 'Osvaldo's music is always wonderfully singable. It has total directness and honesty. Everything comes from the heart.'

PROM 54
7.30pm – c9.50pm

Barber
First Essay for Orchestra   9'

Osvaldo Golijov
Three Songs   23'
UK premiere

interval

Mahler
Symphony No. 5 in C sharp minor   73'

Dawn Upshaw *soprano*

Minnesota Orchestra
Osmo Vänskä *conductor*

Osmo Vänskä

The first of this season's three visiting American orchestras gives the UK premiere of Osvaldo Golijov's *Three Songs*, which they premiered with tonight's soloist in 2002 (see panel, left). Barber's *First Essay* was premiered by Toscanini at the same time as the better-known *Adagio for Strings*. Osmo Vänskä – well-known to Proms audiences from his work with the BBC Scottish Symphony Orchestra – also conducts Mahler's Fifth, whose heart-rending Adagietto was a gift to the composer's wife Alma.

Broadcast on BBC FOUR

📷 **6.00pm Pre-Prom Talk** (RGS)
Roderick Swanston introduces the music of Osvaldo Golijov

PROM 55
7.30pm – c9.35pm

Magnus Lindberg
Sculpture   23'
UK premiere

Mendelssohn
Violin Concerto in E minor   27'

interval

Sibelius
Symphony No. 5 in E flat major   32'

Nikolaj Znaider *violin*

BBC Symphony Orchestra
Jukka-Pekka Saraste *conductor*

Finnish conductor Jukka-Pekka Saraste prefaces his great compatriot Sibelius's soaring Fifth Symphony with the UK premiere of fellow Finn Magnus Lindberg's architecturally inspired new work written for Esa-Pekka Salonen and Los Angeles's new concert hall (see panel, right).

Jukka-Pekka Saraste

Broadcast on BBC FOUR

🎵 **5.30pm Composer Portrait** (RAH)
Magnus Lindberg. See panel, right

Every Prom live on BBC Radio 3 and bbc.co.uk/proms • Advance Booking from 15 May • General Booking from 12 June: 020 7589 8212

90

SATURDAY 26 AUGUST   B

PROM 56

7.00pm – c9.00pm

Ravel
Le tombeau de Couperin   18'

Stravinsky
Violin Concerto   22'

interval

Tchaikovsky
Symphony No. 4 in F minor   42'

Gil Shaham violin

NDR Symphony Orchestra
Christoph von Dohnányi conductor

Gil Shaham

Brilliant violinist Gil Shaham makes an all too rare visit to London for Stravinsky's pithy, neo-Classical concerto. Ravel, too, revisited the past in his elegant dance suite in homage to Couperin. Tchaikovsky grappled with Fate in his Fourth Symphony – 'the force of destiny, which ever prevents our pursuit of happiness from reaching its goal'.

Broadcast on BBC TWO

5.30pm Pre-Prom Panel (RAH)
Broadcasting the Proms
Proms Radio 3 Editor Edward Blakeman, BBC SO Chief Producer Ann McKay, TV Classical Music Editor Oliver Macfarlane and TV director Jonathan Haswell share their insights on bringing the Proms to television and radio

FOCUS ON ... PROM 55
MAGNUS LINDBERG PREMIERE

Martin Anderson on the Finnish composer's musical response to Los Angeles's new concert hall

Magnus Lindberg – still two years short of his half-century – has developed something of a speciality in large orchestral scores that heave with primal energy. *Sculpture*, receiving its UK premiere in Prom 55, is another milestone on the creative road of one of the most fertile imaginations in contemporary music.

In 1984 the explosive power of *Kraft*, Lindberg's last modernist score, set him wondering why modern music had turned its back on the cohesive force of harmony, and from the late 1980s onwards, his compositions began to embrace the best of both worlds, setting the coruscating colours of modernism into a harmonic framework that has all the sense of direction of a Beethoven symphony. This new path led to a towering masterpiece, *Aura*

(1993–4), which Lindberg describes as a 'concerto for orchestra', though it's also a symphony in disguise. That summit achieved, an element of playfulness entered Lindberg's vocabulary – he's a man who likes a good laugh – and the music he has been writing since then miraculously combines a number of opposites: strength and buoyancy, darkness and light, weight and impetus, purpose and levity, as *Sculpture* will demonstrate.

Since Esa-Pekka Salonen, a friend of Lindberg's from their days as fellow students in Helsinki, is the Music Director of the Los Angeles Philharmonic Orchestra, Lindberg was naturally in attendance when, in October 2003, the LA Phil moved into its new home, the Walt Disney Concert Hall *(below)*, designed by

Frank Gehry. Lindberg was deeply impressed by the bold beauty of Gehry's design. *Sculpture* is a tribute to that vision, a monument erected in Lindberg's own material: sound. As if emphasising the idea of construction, *Sculpture* – another symphony *manqué* – is built from the bottom up: Lindberg omits the violins, putting extra weight on the lower registers of the orchestra and throwing the bright and brassy fanfares that animate the piece into sharp relief.

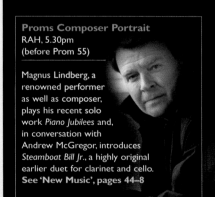

Proms Composer Portrait
RAH, 5.30pm
(before Prom 55)

Magnus Lindberg, a renowned performer as well as composer, plays his recent solo work *Piano Jubilees* and, in conversation with Andrew McGregor, introduces *Steamboat Bill Jr.*, a highly original earlier duet for clarinet and cello.
See 'New Music', pages 44–8

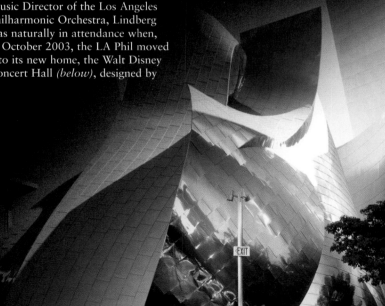

Every Prom live on BBC Radio 3 and bbc.co.uk/proms • Advance Booking from 15 May • General Booking from 12 June: 020 7589 8212

91

FOCUS ON ... PROM 57
MOZART AND MORTALITY

Forget the myths about supernatural visitations from a man in grey, writes **Julian Rushton**. Composing funerary music was all in a day's work for a jobbing musician like Wolfgang Amadeus Mozart

Was Mozart 'much possessed by death'? One might suppose so from letters to his father, written at the time of his mother's death in Paris in 1778 and shortly before Leopold himself died in 1787, in which death is described as 'the goal of our existence' and our truest friend. Mozart's own early death appealed to Romantic sensibilities, and that he left an unfinished *Requiem* provided an irresistible opportunity for myth-making. He foresaw his own death; the *Requiem* was commissioned by a grey stranger, a supernatural visitation; he wrote the *Requiem* for himself ... and so it goes on, even today, with tales of poisoning and a pauper's grave.

Alas, reality must needs intrude on these egregious fantasies. If death was seldom out of Mozart's mind, it

was because death was all around him: four of his six children died in infancy, and some of his younger friends predeceased him. None of this was surprising, given the helplessness of doctors in the face of infectious diseases. The music Mozart wrote in 1791 (the Clarinet concerto, the *Ave verum corpus*) is no more death-devoted than that of earlier years: it may be as much with an eye to the market as to any other consideration that, throughout his life, he contrasted works of passionate, tragic temper – such as the G minor symphony, No. 40 (to be heard in Prom 64) – with works as jovial as its immediate predecessor, No. 39 in E flat major, written in the same summer of 1788.

The E flat symphony is characterised by Mozart's choice of

clarinets instead of the usual oboes. His fondness for the relatively new clarinet family became marked in his Vienna years. Clarinets and basset-horns seem to have featured in the music that enhanced the meetings and ceremonies of the Viennese Masonic lodges, one of which Mozart joined in 1784. Members included many of the aristocrats and intelligentsia of Vienna, and the *Masonic Funeral Music* – to be heard in its reconstructed original version – was composed in 1785 for a memorial event for two of the nobility. Its unique instrumentation includes clarinet, three basset-horns and contrabassoon, with the more usual oboes, horns and strings.

The mournful basset-horns turn up again for the *Requiem*, without oboes, but with trumpets, drums and the trombones usual in sacred choral music. For Mozart, who had spent much of his professional life as a church musician in Salzburg, the commission for a *Requiem* was timely, and not only because of the generous fee; he was preparing to take up a post at St Stephen's Cathedral (though the elderly organist whose shoes he expected to fill outlived him). Had he survived a few more years, we might take a very different view of his output – one much more inclined to German opera (after *The Magic Flute*) and to Catholic church music.

BELOW
Mozart pictured *(far right)* at a Masonic meeting in Vienna, c1784 (painting attributed to Ignaz Unterberger)

PROM 57
7.30pm – c9.30pm

Mozart, reconstr. P. A. Autexier
Meistermusik for men's chorus and orchestra (original version of Masonic Funeral Music, K477)   6'

Mozart
Symphony No. 39 in E flat major, K543   30'

interval

Mozart, compl. Süssmayr
Requiem in D minor, K626   50'

Carolyn Sampson *soprano*
Ingeborg Danz *mezzo-soprano*
Mark Padmore *tenor*
Alfred Reiter *bass*

Collegium Vocale Gent
Orchestre des Champs-Élysées
Philippe Herreweghe *conductor*

Philippe Herreweghe

The first of this Bank Holiday weekend's pair of all-Mozart concerts focuses on music from the last six years of the composer's life *(see panel, left).* Ceremonial music for the passing of fellow brothers of Mozart's Masonic lodge features alongside the Symphony No. 39 in the composer's 'Masonic' key of E flat. Philippe Herreweghe also directs a leading cast in Mozart's valedictory *Requiem*, in the time-honoured completion by the composer's assistant Franz Xaver Süssmayr.

Broadcast on BBC FOUR

6.00pm Pre-Prom Talk (RAH)
Discover the Mozart *Requiem* with Simon Keefe, Professor and Head of Music at City University, London

---

Every Prom live on BBC Radio 3 and bbc.co.uk/proms • Advance Booking from 15 May • General Booking from 12 June: 020 7589 8212

PROM 58
3.30pm – c5.30pm

Ibert
Divertissement   15'

Weill
Songs   10'

Gershwin
Rhapsody in Blue   15'

interval

Dai Fujikura
Crushing Twister   c7'
BBC commission: world premiere

Bernstein
Fancy Free   26'

Kevin Cole piano

BBC Concert Orchestra
Charles Hazlewood conductor/presenter

Charles Hazlewood, the BBC Concert Orchestra's new Principal Guest Conductor, explores how the colours and rhythms of jazz captured the imaginations of a variety of classical composers (see panel, right). Plus a new commission by one of today's brightest young composers. American Gershwin specialist Kevin Cole makes his Proms debut.

Recorded for future broadcast on BBC FOUR

♪ **1.00pm Proms Chamber Music**
See pages 110–13

PROM 59
7.30pm – c9.55pm

Mozart
Symphony No. 34 in C major, K338   22'

Piano Concerto No. 24
in C minor, K491   31'

interval

La finta giardiniera –
'Vorrei punirti, indegno'   4'

Concert aria 'Ch'io mi scordi di te'   11'

Symphony No. 38 in D major,
K504 'Prague'   29'

Véronique Gens soprano
Lars Vogt piano

Salzburg Mozarteum Orchestra
Ivor Bolton conductor

Lars Vogt

As a highlight of this season's Mozart 250th anniversary celebrations, the Salzburg Mozarteum Orchestra – whose foundation can be traced back to Mozart's widow Constanze – performs under British period-performance specialist Ivor Bolton.

Broadcast on BBC FOUR

FOCUS ON ... PROM 58
CHARLES HAZLEWOOD

The BBC Concert Orchestra's new Principal Guest Conductor talks to **Edward Bhesania** about classical music and all that jazz

Familiar to many as a presenter for BBC Television and Radio 3, Charles Hazlewood has chosen the influence of jazz on classical music as the theme of his Bank Holiday matinee – his first Proms appearance as the BBC Concert Orchestra's new Principal Guest Conductor. Not surprisingly, American music figures prominently in the programme. 'In a way jazz was the first truly American musical style,' he explains – 'the first time American composers weren't looking across the pond to Europe for influences.'

Gershwin was undoubtedly the leader of the pack in transferring jazz from the dance hall to the concert hall, and Bernstein used the dance forms of the day to capture the spirit of the times in his 1944 ballet *Fancy Free*, charting 24 hours in the lives of three sailors on shore leave in bustling New York City.

By contrast the 'smoky jazz' of Weill's Weimar years and Ibert's riotous *Divertissement* are what Hazlewood sees as the 'fascinating view of one kind of music through the language of another. In the hands of a great composer, it's bound to achieve something new and distinctive.'

Attempting to blow apart the myth that only certain types of pieces work in family concerts, Hazlewood introduces a new work commissioned from bright talent Dai Fujikura. 'There's a strong Eastern sensibility to his cultural background, which should throw the other pieces into relief. He's got a vivid and fascinating aural imagination that reminds me of a magician's trick-box.'

Hazlewood, who will present as well as conduct the concert, is thrilled about his new relationship with the 'marvellously versatile' BBC Concert Orchestra, whose players, he enthuses, 'might be doing Wagner one day, a Bernstein concert the next day, and backing songwriter Guy Chambers or Brian McFadden from Westlife at the weekend. They throw themselves at everything with a kind of blood-on-the-ceiling commitment.'

Every Prom live on BBC Radio 3 and bbc.co.uk/proms • Advance Booking from 15 May • General Booking from 12 June: 020 7589 8212

93

FOCUS ON ... PROM 61
SIR ANDREW DAVIS

The BBC Symphony Orchestra's Conductor Laureate returns to the Proms with his new American orchestra and an all-American symphony

Long before becoming Music Director of the Chicago Lyric Opera in 2000, Sir Andrew Davis *(left)* had explored the music of American maverick Charles Ives *(below)* in a memorable Barbican weekend with the BBC Symphony Orchestra. This year he brings Ives's early Second Symphony to the Proms, with the Pittsburgh Symphony Orchestra, of which he became Artistic Advisor this season.

Like John Adams's *My Father Knew Charles Ives* (see Prom 38), the symphony is a musical memoir of a small-town New England upbringing. Hymn tunes, patriotic songs and marches drift in and out, alongside the European influences of Brahms, Bach, Wagner, Dvořák and others.

'There is not much to say about the symphony,' said Ives of the work. 'It expresses the musical feelings of the Connecticut country around here in the 1890s, the music of the country folk. It is full of the tunes they sang and played then.'

'When I first heard the piece, it knocked me out,' remembers Davis, 'and I suddenly got into American music. It's extraordinarily original. It's a great example of a man trying to pour his innovative ideas into a form that is theoretically conventional. But for all its "homely" feel – and there's a strong whiff of New England Transcendentalism – it's a piece that comes across in a great big sweep.'

He describes his new orchestra – with which he will spend five to six weeks a year – as one that boasts 'great exuberance of expression and commitment. They have fantastic solo players and a deeply intense sound that I love. Like many American cities, Pittsburgh is very sports-oriented – keen on their football, baseball and hockey – and it's wonderful that the orchestra's audience has that sports-fan kind of zeal too.'

PROM 60
7.30pm – c9.40pm

Hans Werner Henze
Five Messages for the Queen of Sheba   20'
London premiere

interval

Shostakovich
Symphony No. 7 in C major, 'Leningrad'   75'

Orchestre National de France
Kurt Masur *conductor*

Kurt Masur conducts the London premiere of Henze's *Five Messages*, which draws on motifs from his latest opera, *L'Upupa*, about a magical bird charged with carrying messages between King Solomon and the Queen of Sheba. Shostakovich's 'Leningrad' Symphony – written in the city while it was under German siege – carried a powerful message to the outside world of the USSR's struggle against Nazism.

Broadcast on BBC FOUR

📺 **6.00pm Pre-Prom Talk** (RAH)
Piers Burton-Page introduces Henze's *Five Messages for the Queen of Sheba*

PROM 61
7.30pm – c9.45pm

Ives
Symphony No. 2   38'

interval

Chopin
Piano Concerto No. 1 in E minor   39'

R. Strauss
Till Eulenspiegel   15'

Lang Lang *piano*

Pittsburgh Symphony Orchestra
Sir Andrew Davis *conductor*

In his first season as Artistic Advisor of the Pittsburgh Symphony, Sir Andrew Davis crosses the pond with Ives's early, Romantically inclined kaleidoscope of American songs and melodies *(see panel, left)*. One of the most celebrated of young pianists, Lang Lang returns to the Proms following his exciting First Night performance in 2003. The merry pranks of Strauss's *Till Eulenspiegel* promise to put the orchestra through its paces.

Every Prom live on BBC Radio 3 and bbc.co.uk/proms • Advance Booking from 15 May • General Booking from 12 June: 020 7589 8212

94

PROM 62

7.00pm – c9.05pm

Mozart
Piano Concerto No. 23
in A major, K488   26'

interval

Bruckner
Symphony No. 9 in D minor   65'

Richard Goode *piano*

BBC Symphony Orchestra
Jiří Bělohlávek *conductor*

Richard Goode

The BBC SO's new Chief Conductor
directs Bruckner's spiritual swansong *(see
panel, right)*, prefaced by Mozart's dramatic
Piano Concerto in A major, to which
American pianist Richard Goode should
bring his characteristic insight.

Broadcast on BBC FOUR

FOCUS ON ... PROM 62

BRUCKNER: SYMPHONY NO. 9

Had Bruckner lived just a few weeks longer, he would surely have completed his Ninth Symphony. Yet, as
Stephen Johnson says, the three-movement torso still provides a suitable spiritual finale to his life and art

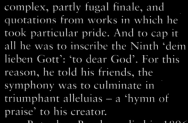

Bruckner knew that his Ninth
Symphony was to be his last. 'I shall
write nine symphonies,' he told one
of his classes at the Vienna University,
'and the Ninth shall be in D minor,
like Beethoven's – Beethoven won't
object.' It was to be the summation
of his life's achievement, with a grand,

complex, partly fugal finale, and
quotations from works in which he
took particular pride. And to cap it
all he was to inscribe the Ninth 'dem
lieben Gott': 'to dear God'. For this
reason, he told his friends, the
symphony was to culminate in
triumphant alleluias – a 'hymn of
praise' to his creator.

But when Bruckner died in 1896
– nine years after he started work on
the symphony – only the first three
movements were complete. What then
of that all-important finale? Bruckner's
executors were confronted with piles
of sketches and a fair quantity of
fully orchestrated material; but of
that crucial hymn-like conclusion,
nothing. So the decision was taken
to perform the three completed
movements as they stood. It was soon
discovered that the Ninth Symphony
worked rather well in this apparently
incomplete state – like the two
surviving movements of Schubert's
'Unfinished' Symphony. The Adagio
third movement made a remarkably
poignant ending, with its final loving
glance back to the opening of the
Seventh Symphony, the warmest and
most serene of his purely orchestral
works (to be heard in Prom 65).
And hadn't Bruckner referred to
this Adagio as his 'Farewell to Life'?
Very soon a myth grew up: Bruckner
hadn't finished the finale of the Ninth

because he couldn't. The loud
affirmation he intended wasn't
appropriate, and his imagination
had simply failed him.

It's a comforting story, but it's
almost certainly untrue. We have an
account by a key witness who heard
Bruckner play the end of the
symphony, and Bruckner's biographer
Max Auer insisted that he saw a page
at or near the end of the finale, which
then disappeared. The painful truth
is that Bruckner was probably only
within a few weeks of completing the
score when he died. Almost certainly
he had the final pages on his bedside
table, and it would have been these
crucial pages to which some of the
numerous souvenir-hunters helped
themselves after his death.

A few sketches of the ending have
turned up, but tantalisingly they give
only a rough outline. So the finale of
Bruckner's Ninth looks likely to
remain one of the great 'might-have-
beens' of music. Yet those three
complete movements as they stand
form a gripping and deeply moving
testimony to Bruckner's last great
spiritual struggle. And, however
much one knows about the fate
of that finale, it is still possible to
believe, as the great Adagio fades
into silence, that the Ninth Symphony
as we know it ends on the verge of
the inexpressible.

Every Prom live on BBC Radio 3 and bbc.co.uk/proms • Advance Booking from 15 May • General Booking from 12 June: 020 7589 8212

95

KURTÁG AND FELDMAN

Calum MacDonald contrasts two modern masters – a Hungarian miniaturist and an American maximalist – both born 80 years ago

Morton Feldman and György Kurtág are among the great musical individualists of the past 50 years, and their joint 80th-birthday concert (Feldman died in 1987, but Kurtág is happily still with us) shows each composer at his most inimitable. Their approaches to their art seem utterly opposed. Feldman's proceeded from his appreciation of the visual arts, whether 1950s New York Expressionism or the patient arts of Turkish rug-makers. For him, the musical work was a canvas to be filled or a frieze to be drawn, sometimes to enormous length: time does not seem to matter, or even to exist, in his music. Time is precious to Kurtág, a natural miniaturist, indeed an aphorist. A cell of a few notes can be an entire work, or the start of a much larger cycle accumulated from a whole collection of such miniatures. Yet both composers can evoke an intense mood of elegy.

Composed for the 1971 dedication of the Rothko Chapel at the University of St Thomas in Houston, Texas, which is structured around Mark Rothko's huge, almost monochrome canvases, Feldman's *Rothko Chapel* (which marks the Proms debut of the composer's music) is also a memorial to the artist, a personal friend of many years, who had recently committed suicide. A dreamlike inner landscape is created, meditative and spiritual without any religious specificity: the voices have no words.

Words are of great significance for Kurtág, who has said that Russian is for him a 'sacred' language; he learnt it in order to read Dostoyevsky and it has deeply affected him since. Fourteen years in the making, *Songs of Despair and Sorrow* is both plangent and lyrically monumental. It sets poems by Lermontov, Mandelstam, Akhmatova and others for chorus and an extraordinary ensemble of two harmoniums, brass quintet, string sextet, two harps, four bayans (accordions) and percussion.

LEFT
The 'inner landscape' of the Rothko Chapel, Houston, Texas

György Kurtág
Songs of Despair and Sorrow   21'

Schumann
Four Songs for double chorus, Op. 141*   5'

Feldman
Rothko Chapel   27'

Amy Freston *soprano*

BBC Singers
Nash Ensemble
Martyn Brabbins *conductor*
Stephen Cleobury *conductor**

In a late-night concert devoted to three of this year's anniversary composers, the BBC Singers contrast Feldman's characteristically slow and expansive tribute to Mark Rothko, written a year after the artist had killed himself, with Kurtág's settings of texts by ill-fated Russian poets, two of whom also took their own lives *(see panel, left)*.

György Kurtág

Morton Feldman

There will be no interval

Mozart
Symphony No. 25 in G minor, K183   23'

Hanspeter Kyburz
Noesis   22'
London premiere

interval

Debussy, orch. Colin Matthews
Préludes (Book 2) – 'Ce qu'a vu le vent d'ouest'; 'Feuilles mortes'; 'Feux d'artifice'   15'

Mozart
Symphony No. 40 in G minor, K550   30'

Berliner Philharmoniker
Sir Simon Rattle *conductor*

Sir Simon Rattle

Sir Simon Rattle returns to the Proms to give Mozart the Berlin treatment in a highlight of our celebration of the composer's 250th anniversary. Fellow anniversary composer Colin Matthews (60 this year) reworks three of Debussy's impressionistic piano *Préludes* and, ever the champion of new music, Rattle brings Berlin-based Hanspeter Kyburz's gritty *Noesis*, whose New York premiere he conducted earlier this year at Carnegie Hall *(see panel, right)*.

Broadcast on BBC FOUR

Every Prom live on BBC Radio 3 and bbc.co.uk/proms • Advance Booking from 15 May • General Booking from 12 June: 020 7589 8212

96

PROM 72

7.30pm – c9.45pm

Mozart
Symphony No. 35 in D major,
K385 'Haffner'   20'

interval

Mozart, compl. Robert D. Levin
Mass in C minor, K427   85'
UK premiere of this version

Rosemary Joshua *soprano*
Lisa Milne *soprano*
Eric Cutler *tenor*
Nathan Berg *bass-baritone*

Choir of the Enlightenment
Orchestra of the Age
of Enlightenment
Sir Charles Mackerras *conductor*

Sir Charles Mackerras

In the final instalment of this season's Mozart-anniversary survey Sir Charles Mackerras pairs one of the composer's earliest Viennese symphonies, written for the ennoblement of a family friend back in Salzburg, with his late, great Mass, apparently begun to celebrate his marriage to Constanze but unaccountably never completed. It is here performed in the scholar-pianist Robert D. Levin's exciting new edition, premiered last year in New York *(see panel, right)*.

Broadcast on BBC FOUR

🎙 **6.00pm Pre-Prom Talk** (RAH)
Discover more about Mozart's C minor Mass with BBC Radio 3's Mark Lowther

---

FOCUS ON ... PROM 72
MOZART: MASS IN C MINOR

No-one can ever know for certain why Mozart didn't complete his great C minor Mass but the pianist-scholar **Robert D. Levin** thinks he's taken a pretty educated guess as to how the composer might have done so, if he'd tried

Two major mysteries surround Mozart's great Mass in C minor – the first is why he began it; the second is why he never finished it. In a letter to his father Leopold, dated 4 January 1783, Mozart implies that he embarked upon the Mass in fulfilment of a vow but leaves it unclear whether this vow related to his marriage to Constanze – against his father's will – the previous August, to her recovery from a serious illness shortly before the wedding, or to the hoped-for arrival of their first child – little Leopold, born on 17 June 1783. If it was the latter (as Constanze herself always later claimed), then little Leopold's death in August, while his parents were away on their first visit together to see Leopold senior in Salzburg, might have been reason enough for Mozart to abandon the score – though it might equally well have been the reformist Emperor Joseph II's ban on the excessive use of music in church. Either way, the C minor Mass was actually performed, incomplete as it was, in St Peter's Church, Salzburg, on 26 October 1783 with Constanze as one of the soprano soloists.

At once a sign that Mozart never intended completing the Mass and a pointer to the manner in which he might well have done so, if he had ever tried, is the fact that two years later, in March 1785, he refitted the fragments to a new Italian text for the biblical cantata *Davidde penitente* ('The Penitent David'), recycling the completed Kyrie and Gloria of the Mass and adding two new arias, one each for tenor and soprano.

It is these two arias that gave pianist-musicologist Robert D. Levin the clue he needed to proceed, once he had finally been persuaded by German conductor Helmuth Rilling to follow up his 1991 bicentenary-year edition of the *Requiem* by completing Mozart's other unfinished Mass. 'For, lo and behold, the music of these arias fits exactly with the Latin text of the missing "Et in Spiritum Sanctum" and "Agnus Dei".' Surviving sketches from 1783 were used to plug other gaps.

But why even try to complete it, when the unfinished score is so lovely as it is? 'Because this is not a concert work,' says Levin, 'this is a Catholic Mass – a musical expression of Christian faith. As such, it's very odd indeed for it not to include either crucifixion, resurrection or the hope of the life to come.' And now it does, in a version he can honestly claim to be '100% Mozart'.

BELOW
Constanze Mozart: portrait by her brother-in-law Joseph Lange, 1782

Every Prom live on BBC Radio 3 and bbc.co.uk/proms • Advance Booking from 15 May • General Booking from 12 June: 020 7589 8212

101

F

FOCUS ON ... PROM 73
MARK ELDER: THE MAESTRO MIX

Almost 20 years after he last conducted a Last Night of the Proms, Mark Elder returns to preside over an evening that still remains unlike any other in the concert calendar. **Louise Downes** reports

It was 1987 when Mark Elder, then riding high as Music Director of ENO, last conducted a Last Night of the Proms. Things have moved on a lot since then, both for him – he's now enjoying deservedly great success as Music Director of the Hallé in Manchester – and for the Last Night itself. For while the event's popular pot-pourri format still preserves the last vestiges of what Henry Wood's original Proms would have been like back in 1895, the onward march of technology has taken the traditional element of impromptu audience participation to a whole new level. Says Elder: 'As the conductor of the Last Night, you're not just controlling the forces on stage, but interacting with the audience as well. You have to be on your toes for anything that might happen. And now, with the involvement of all the Proms in the Park events around the country, I gather you have to act as a sort of Master of Ceremonies too, bringing all these different elements together.'

But the really important thing, he stresses, is to get the programme right – 'with the right mix of items, both good music done as well as possible and party-pieces done just for fun, so that it all adds up to a satisfying concert as well as a festive end to the season.' With no Mozart ('we didn't feel obliged to tick all the anniversary boxes') but a 'brilliant' Shostakovich curtain-raiser ('his wicked take-off of the *Ruslan and Lyudmila* overture'), relative rarities like the Eric Coates march, a good old-fashioned Wagnerian 'bleeding chunk' and two star Russian soloists to provide a moment or two of stillness in the first half ('since celebratory needn't mean relentlessly upbeat'), Elder is hoping he's got the mix just about right.

Every Prom live on BBC Radio 3 and bbc.co.uk/proms • Advance Booking from 15 May • General Booking from 12 June: 020 7589 8212

102

PROM 73
7.30pm – c10.35pm

THE LAST NIGHT OF THE PROMS 2006

Shostakovich
Festive Overture   6'

Borodin
Prince Igor – 'No sleep, no rest'   7'

Verdi
Ernani – 'Gran dio! …
Oh de' verd'anni miei'   5'

Rubinstein
Nero – Epithalamium   2'

Colin Matthews
Vivo   5'

Prokofiev
Violin Concerto No. 2 in G minor   27'

Wagner
Tannhäuser – Entry of the Guests   6'

interval

Coates
March 'Calling All Workers'   3'

Bizet
Carmen – Toreador's Song   6'

Soloviev-Sedoy
Moscow Nights   4'

Violin solo, **arr. Matthew Barley**   c5'
world premiere

Elgar
Pomp and Circumstance March No. 1
in D major ('Land of Hope and Glory') 8'

Henry Wood
Fantasia on British Sea-Songs
(with additional numbers
arr. Bob Chilcott)   24'

Parry, orch. Elgar
Jerusalem   2'

The National Anthem   2'

Auld Lang Syne   2'

Dmitri Hvorostovsky *baritone*
Viktoria Mullova *violin*

BBC Singers
BBC Symphony Chorus
BBC Symphony Orchestra
Mark Elder *conductor*

In Shostakovich's centenary year, there is a Russian flavour to the Last Night with two outstanding soloists performing classics of the vocal and violin repertory, while conductor Mark Elder returns with favourite composers – Verdi and Wagner – a famous radio melody and a contemporary classic. The final sequence draws the four nations of the UK together in a classic celebration of music-making.

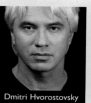
Dmitri Hvorostovsky

Viktoria Mullova

Broadcast on BBC TWO (Part 1) and BBC ONE (Part 2)

Celebrate the Last Night across the UK

BBC PROMS in the Park

Join in the festivities throughout the UK for the party of the year as once again Proms in the Park in Belfast, Glasgow, London, Manchester and Swansea celebrate the Last Night of the BBC Proms.

See overleaf for full details

Events sponsored by

national savings & investments

ns&i

Join us in venues around the UK for the party of the year!

BBC PROMS in the Park

Each Prom in the Park features a live concert with celebrity presenters and performers followed by a live big screen link-up to events in the Royal Albert Hall. Pack up a picnic and gather up your friends for a chance to join in the traditional Last Night singalong and a great night out.

Alternatively, you can join in the festivities at the BBC Big Screens in Birmingham (Chamberlain Square), Hull (Victoria Square), Liverpool (Clayton Square) and Manchester (Exchange Square) and this year, in Leeds (Millennium Square) for the first time.

This year's concerts are broadcast live across BBC Radio and Television: BBC Radio 2 broadcasts from London's Hyde Park; BBC Radio Ulster, BBC Radio Scotland, BBC Radio Manchester and BBC Radio Wales broadcast their local events from Belfast, Glasgow, Manchester and Swansea. Highlights of all five Proms in the Park concerts will be included as part of the live coverage of the Last Night on BBC ONE and BBC TWO, while Digital TV viewers can choose between watching proceedings inside the Royal Albert Hall and the various Proms in the Park concerts taking place across the UK.

Events sponsored by

national savings & investments

ns&i

Note that all BBC Proms in the Park events are outdoors and tickets are unreserved. The use of chairs is discouraged since it obstructs the view of others, but if you find it necessary because of limited mobility, please be considerate to your neighbours. In the interest of safety, please do not bring glass items, barbecues or flaming torches.

PROMS IN THE PARK

Hyde Park, London

Angela Gheorghiu *soprano*
Alison Balsom *trumpet*
Terry Wogan *presenter*

THE ROYAL PARKS

Royal Choral Society
BBC Concert Orchestra
Carl Davis *conductor*

Terry Wogan

Alison Balsom

The inimitable Terry Wogan hosts the celebrations in Hyde Park, where performers include international opera star Angela Gheorghiu and brilliant trumpeter Alison Balsom, accompanied by Proms in the Park favourites, the BBC Concert Orchestra, conducted by Carl Davis. Radio 2's Ken Bruce gets the proceedings under way with music from old favourites Chas & Dave and Madness tribute band One Step Behind.

Gates open 4.00pm.
Entertainment on stage from 5.30pm.

For corporate hospitality facilities, call Charles Webb on 0870 720 3010 or visit www.arenaevents.com

Angela Gheorghiu

Tickets: £23.00 (under-3s free), available now by post/fax using the Booking Form *(facing page 142)*, by phone on 0870 899 8100 (24 hours, national rate) or online at bbc.co.uk/proms, and also (after 13 June) from the Royal Albert Hall on 020 7589 8212 (9.00am–9.00pm).
A £2.50 transaction fee applies.

Tickets can also be bought in person (no transaction fee) from the BBC Shops at 50 Margaret Street, London W1, Bush House, Strand, London WC2 and Fife Road, Kingston.

Advance Booking from 15 May • General Booking from 12 June: 020 7589 8212 • Online booking bbc.co.uk/proms

PROMS IN THE PARK

Donegall Square, Belfast

Ailish Tynan *soprano*
Noel Thompson *presenter*

Ulster Orchestra
Kenneth Montgomery *conductor*

Once again, the grounds of Belfast's City Hall provide the setting for the Last Night festivities in Northern Ireland as award-winning news anchorman Noel Thompson presents a thrilling evening of music from the Ulster Orchestra and guests including the outstanding young Irish soprano Ailish Tynan.

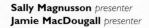
Ailish Tynan

Donegall Square

For full details call 0870 333 1918, textphone 08000 153350, or visit bbc.co.uk/ni/tickets

PROMS IN THE PARK

Glasgow Green

Sally Magnusson *presenter*
Jamie MacDougall *presenter*

Inverclyde Junior Choir
BBC Scottish Symphony Orchestra

Join us for an unforgettable and spectacular evening north of the border, as we celebrate the Last Night of the Proms in true Scottish style with the BBC Scottish Symphony Orchestra.

Sally Magnusson

Glasgow Green

For full details call 08700 100160 or visit bbc.co.uk/proms

PROMS IN THE PARK

Heaton Park, Manchester

BBC Philharmonic
Steve Bell *conductor*

BBC Proms in the Park returns to Manchester's beautifully restored Heaton Park with a magnificent outdoor classical music concert featuring the world-renowned BBC Philharmonic and very special guests.

Bring along a picnic and enjoy a night of unforgettable magic. The popular classics will be accompanied by stunning fireworks before a spectacular live link-up to the Royal Albert Hall gives you the chance to sing along to those Last Night favourites.

Heaton Park

Tickets: £12.50 (under-12s free with accompanying adult), available now from Manchester Visitor Information Centre in St Peter's Square (0871 2228 223), in person at Heaton Park Farm Centre (cash/cheque only) or online at bbc.co.uk/proms (75p handling charge)

PROMS IN THE PARK

Singleton Park, Swansea

Aled Jones *presenter*

BBC National Chorus of Wales
BBC National Orchestra of Wales
Eric Stern *conductor*

Aled Jones presents a night of magical music under the stars as Wales joins the annual Last Night of the Proms celebrations. With the traditional audience participation, big screen link-up and spectacular fireworks, this will be a night to remember.

Aled Jones

Singleton Park

Tickets: £7.50 in advance, £10.00 on the night (under-12s free with accompanying adult), available from the BBC Call NOW Line on 08700 13 1812 and in person or by phone from the Grand Theatre, Singleton Street, Swansea (01792 475715)

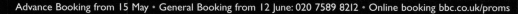
Advance Booking from 15 May • General Booking from 12 June: 020 7589 8212 • Online booking bbc.co.uk/proms

BBC SCOTTISH SYMPHONY ORCHESTRA

Glasgow City Halls, new home of the BBC Scottish Symphony Orchestra

"One of the finest halls anywhere in the country"

TOM SERVICE, THE GUARDIAN

"The BBC Scottish Symphony Orchestra… what a remarkable outfit the band has become, particularly under the leadership of the charismatic young Israeli conductor Ilan Volkov… The orchestra is firing on all cylinders." GEORGE HALL, THE OBSERVER

CHIEF CONDUCTOR ILAN VOLKOV

Associate Guest Conductor   **Stefan Solyom**
Composer in Association   **Jonathan Harvey**
Composer in Residence   **Anna Meredith**

For information about the BBC SSO's concerts, broadcasts and activities, please visit
bbc.co.uk/bbcsso

BBC Proms at Cadogan Hall

Cadogan Hall

5 Sloane Terrace, London SW1

(see map, page 136)

www.cadoganhall.com

Following the success of last season's Proms Chamber Music series in its new venue at Cadogan Hall, this season we launch a new experiment: four Saturday matinee concerts highlighting the music of this year's anniversary composers Mozart and Shostakovich in performances by leading British chamber orchestras. Proms Chamber Music meanwhile welcomes artists from both home and abroad, featuring distinguished visitors from across Europe alongside the best of young British performers, many of them current or former members of BBC Radio 3's New Generation Artists scheme.

Proms Saturday Matinee (PSM) and Proms Chamber Music (PCM) concerts are broadcast live on BBC Radio 3

Proms Chamber Music concerts are also repeated the following Saturday at 12.00 noon

Doors will open at 11.45am (PCMs) and 1.45pm (PSMs); entrance to the auditorium will be from half an hour before start-time

PLUS
The Adverb

Mondays, 2.15pm (immediately after Proms Chamber Music concerts)

Poetry and prose in performance. Featured authors join Ian McMillan and guest presenters for classic writings on music and specially commissioned new pieces.
Admission free to PCM ticket-holders.
Recorded for broadcast on BBC Radio 3 during Proms intervals on Thursdays

Ticket Prices at Cadogan Hall

PROMS SATURDAY MATINEES (PSM)
Stalls: £15.00; Centre Gallery: £12.00

PROMS CHAMBER MUSIC (PCM)
Stalls: £10.00; Centre Gallery: £8.00

DAY SEATS (BOTH SERIES)
Side Gallery: £5.00

Advance Booking, from Monday 15 May
To book tickets during the Advance Booking period, use the Booking Form *(facing page 142)* or the Online Ticket Request system (at bbc.co.uk/proms)

General Booking, from Monday 12 June
Once General Booking has opened, you can also book tickets by telephone or in person at the Royal Albert Hall (on 020 7589 8212) or at Cadogan Hall (on 020 7730 4500), as well as online.

Any Stalls or Centre Gallery tickets still available on the day of the concert can only be bought at Cadogan Hall, from 10.00am.

£5.00 tickets on the day
At least 150 Side Gallery (bench) seats will be available for just £5.00 each on the day of the concert. These tickets can only be bought at Cadogan Hall, from 10.00am. They must be purchased in person and with cash only, and are limited to two tickets per transaction.

£25.00 PCM Series Pass
Hear all eight PCM concerts for just £25.00, with guaranteed entrance to the Side Gallery until 12.50pm (after which PCM Pass-holders may be asked to join the day queue).

During the Advance Booking period (from Monday 15 May), PCM Series Passes can be purchased using the Booking Form *(facing page 142)* or the Online Ticket Request system (at bbc.co.uk/proms).

Once General Booking has opened (on Monday 12 June), PCM Series Passes can also be purchased by telephone or in person at the Royal Albert Hall (on 020 7589 8212) as well as online.

PCM Passes are subject to availability.

Every Prom live on BBC Radio 3 and bbc.co.uk/proms • Advance Booking from 15 May • General Booking from 12 June: 020 7589 8212

107

FOCUS ON ... PSM 3

SHOSTAKOVICH AT THE MOVIES

John Riley fast forwards through the composer's film career

Shostakovich's involvement with the cinema extended from accompanying silent films in 1923 to scoring *King Lear* in 1970, and his work on around three dozen films marked all his other music, as he bounced ideas from the cinema to the concert hall and back again.

After escaping the cinema pit, he was lured back to write an orchestral score for *New Babylon* (1929), Kozintsev and Trauberg's film about the Paris Commune. It was the start of a fruitful relationship with the directors but a troubled one with cinema. *New Babylon*'s music and images

reflected ironically off each other, but political and artistic problems led to a fiasco and Shostakovich never revived it, though it is one of his most characteristic early scores and irony was one of the mainstays of his future career.

Just like his concert works, his early film scores are full of innovative sounds and structural ideas: for an animated version of Pushkin's *The Tale of the Priest and His Servant Blockhead* (1933–5) Shostakovich matched the stark, folk-like images with pungent, farcical music typical of his early style. But the attack on his opera *Lady Macbeth of the Mtsensk District* (Prom 49) forced him to take less interesting cinema work simply to survive the late 1930s.

Cinematically, he had a quiet war (the charming *Silly Little Mouse* just preceded the USSR's entry) but after his 1948 denunciation he had to work on a stream of Sovietised histories and biopics and Stalinist hagiographies. Yet even here he was able to revisit ideas in different contexts, using the cinema as a crucible for his other work.

In later years he saved his cinematic energy for collaborations with close friends, including Kozintsev, with whom he made *Hamlet* (see Proms Films, page 120) in 1963 and *King Lear*, both men's last film, six years later.

PSM 1
3.00pm – c4.45pm

Schnittke
Moz-Art à la Haydn   12'

Mozart
Symphony No. 14 in A major, K114   20'
Serenade in D major, K250 'Haffner'   58'

David Juritz *violin*

London Mozart Players
Isabelle van Keulen *director/violin*

Isabelle van Keulen

Isabelle van Keulen directs the London Mozart Players in a symphony and a serenade from Mozart's Salzburg years, prefaced with a musical joke by Alfred Schnittke that plays – almost to death – a fragment of Mozartian pantomime music in a comic homage whose 'Haydn' twist is amusingly linked to the 'Surprise' Symphony (see Prom 14).

There will be no interval

PSM 2
3.00pm – c4.15pm

J. S. Bach
Brandenburg Concerto No. 4
in G major, BWV 1049   16'

Mozart
Divertimento in D major, K136   12'
Adagio and Fugue in C minor, K546   8'

J. S. Bach
Brandenburg Concerto No. 5
in D major, BWV 1050   21'

Rachel Brown *flute/recorder*
Rachel Beckett *recorder*
Pavlo Beznosiuk *violin*

The Academy of Ancient Music
Richard Egarr *harpsichord/director*

The Academy of Ancient Music under its new Associate Director Richard Egarr gives Bach and Mozart the period-instrument treatment. Mozart's majestic fugue-writing in his *Adagio and Fugue* celebrates 'this most artistic and beautiful of musical forms', while the concert is framed by a pair of Brandenburg Concertos by the master of fugue himself.

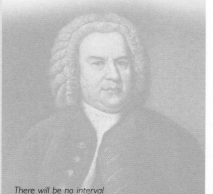

There will be no interval

Every Prom live on BBC Radio 3 and bbc.co.uk/proms • Advance Booking from 15 May • General Booking from 12 June: 020 7589 8212

108

SATURDAY 19 AUGUST	**SATURDAY 2 SEPTEMBER**

PSM 3
3.00pm – c4.30pm

Shostakovich

Jazz Suite No. 1	7'
New Babylon – excerpt	12'
Five Fragments for Orchestra, Op. 42	9'
The Tale of the Priest and His Servant Blockhead – excerpts	10'
The Bedbug – excerpts	10'
The Silly Little Mouse	16'

Britten Sinfonia
André de Ridder *conductor*

New Babylon

Live performances of three of Shostakovich's most original film scores, including two for children's cartoons – and all accompanied by original film footage – plus selections from his uproarious score for the savage theatrical satire *The Bedbug* and some light music too *(see panel, left)*.

There will be no interval

PSM 4
3.00pm – c4.30pm

Mozart

The Magic Flute – Overture	7'

Benjamin Wallfisch

New work *world premiere*	c7'

Mozart

Serenade in G major, K525 'Eine kleine Nachtmusik'	18'
Thamos, King of Egypt – incidental music, K345 *(sung in German)*	40'

OSJ Voices
OSJ
John Lubbock *conductor*

A rare chance to hear Mozart's only incidental music for the theatre *(see panel, right)*. The light-hearted 'Little Night Music', containing the most-whistled of all Mozart's themes, contrasts with a new work by the OSJ's Associate Composer, Benjamin Wallfisch.

There will be no interval

FOCUS ON ... PSM 4
MOZART AT THE THEATRE

Rupert Christiansen relishes the precocious musical ambition apparent in a rarely heard Mozartian theatre score that anticipates the Egyptian setting and solemn majesty of the later *Magic Flute*

Mozart adored the theatre, and as a young man he always jumped at any chance to compose for it, whether the frame was opera, ballet or drama. The incidental music he wrote for Baron von Gebler's long-forgotten play *Thamos, King of Egypt* constitutes one of the most intriguing oddities of his *oeuvre*. For this two-dimensional heroic drama of whitest good pitched against blackest evil, set in ancient Heliopolis, he provided three choruses (one with a solemn baritone solo) and five orchestral interludes, the fourth of which was intended as accompaniment for a highly declamatory speech. There is much stormy agitation and chromatic intensity in the interludes, but it is the choruses that are more remarkable: richly orchestrated and brightly exultant in tone, they are underpinned by a sinewy, masculine energy that is a world away from the rococo delicacy of *Eine kleine Nachtmusik* and that has reminded some critics of the Masonic elements in *The Magic Flute*.

All sorts of guesswork surround the composition. The music for *Thamos*'s first production in 1773 (by one Johann Sattler) seems to have been dumped, and Mozart appears to have been called in to write two replacement choruses for its Viennese revival the following year, adding the third chorus and the interludes in 1776–7, and then revising all the numbers for another production in 1779. But all this can only be surmised from analysis of paper and handwriting, and the dating of the music is still the subject of much scholarly debate. None of this need worry the concert-goer, however, who can instantly enjoy a score that shows the young Mozart's Classicism at its most bracingly grand and ambitious.

BELOW
The Magic Flute: set design by Karl Friedrich Schinkel for the Berlin Opera, 1816

Every Prom live on BBC Radio 3 and bbc.co.uk/proms • Advance Booking from 15 May • General Booking from 12 June: 020 7589 8212

109

FOCUS ON ... PCM 2
ROYAL & RICE

David Gillard introduces two young singers making their duo debut together in this year's Proms Chamber Music series

When two of Britain's most acclaimed young opera stars get together for their first joint recital, you can be sure of a memorable occasion. And when they happen to be the best of friends, too, you may expect some very special chemistry. So there's much to look forward to when soprano Kate Royal *(above)* and mezzo-soprano Christine Rice *(below)* join forces for the second of this year's Proms Chamber Music concerts at Cadogan Hall.

It was the Proms that first brought them together two years ago when they both sang Rhinemaidens in Sir Simon Rattle's concert

performance of Wagner's *Das Rheingold*. 'We got on like a house on fire,' recalls Christine. 'I'd heard Kate on Radio 3 when she won the Kathleen Ferrier Award and thought then: "She seems nice – and what a voice!"' And Kate remembers: 'I'd admired Christine's voice from her work as a Radio 3 New Generation Artist and we soon discovered that we shared a natural attitude to the way we produce our voices – we don't put effect on top of what is already there.'

Within the past year they've appeared together in Britten's *A Midsummer Night's Dream* in Madrid and rehearsed together for the Glyndebourne tour, when Kate sang the Countess in Mozart's *The Marriage of Figaro* and Christine the title-role in Rossini's *La Cenerentola*. Though both have largely made their names in opera, they have already begun to establish their reputations as superb recitalists. But a duet recital is something new. So are we looking at the Ann Murray and Felicity Lott of the younger generation? They wouldn't dream of making such an illustrious comparison but they do say: 'We very much hope it's a partnership that endures.'

PCM 1
1.00pm – c2.00pm

Schumann
Three Romances for oboe
and piano, Op. 94   13'

Stravinsky
Three Pieces for solo clarinet   5'

Poulenc
Sonata for clarinet and bassoon   7'

Mozart
Quintet in E flat major for piano
and wind, K452   24'

Christoph Eschenbach *piano*

Solistes de l'Orchestre de Paris
  Alexandre Gattet *oboe*
  Philippe Berrod *clarinet*
  Michel Garcin-Marrou *horn*
  Marc Trenel *bassoon*

Putting aside his baton after Wagner's *Siegfried* (Prom 3), Christoph Eschenbach returns to two of his first musical loves: the piano and Mozart. He is joined by principal players from his Paris orchestra in

Christoph Eschenbach

Mozart's bravura Quintet, and they also pay tribute to anniversary composer Schumann and explore the crisp wind sonorities of Stravinsky and Poulenc.

There will be no interval

🔲 **2.15pm The Adverb** (CH)
See page 107

PCM 2
1.00pm – c2.00pm

Programme to include songs and duets by Purcell, Mozart, Mendelssohn, Gounod, Chausson and Brahms

Kate Royal *soprano*
Christine Rice *mezzo-soprano*
Roger Vignoles *piano*

A first chance to savour the delights of a new musical partnership, born of the enjoyment these two young star singers have had recently working together in opera *(see panel, left)*. They are partnered by a renowned pianist with a great love of the repertoire as they set off on a musical journey of adventure through several centuries of duet songbooks.

There will be no interval

🔲 **2.15pm The Adverb** (CH)
See page 107

Every Prom live on BBC Radio 3 and bbc.co.uk/proms • Advance Booking from 15 May • General Booking from 12 June: 020 7589 8212

110

PCM 3

1.00pm – c2.00pm

Mozart
String Quartet in B flat major,
K458 'Hunt'   22'

Shostakovich
String Quartet No. 7   15'

Szymanowski
String Quartet No. 2   18'

Royal String Quartet
Izabella Szalaj-Zimak *violin*
Elwira Przybylowska *violin*
Marek Czech *viola*
Michal Pepol *cello*

Shostakovich and his wife Nina

Four brilliant young Polish players unlock the power and beauty of the music of fellow countryman Szymanowski in a programme that also salutes the uniquely original imagination of Mozart, and celebrates Shostakovich's anniversary with one of his most personal quartets – a bittersweet tribute to his first wife.

There will be no interval

🔊 **2.15pm The Adverb** (CH)
See page 107

PCM 4

1.00pm – c2.00pm

Schumann
Dichterliebe, Op. 48   30'
Lieder, Op. 40 – selections   10'
Lieder und Gesänge, Op. 98a –
selections   9'

Christian Gerhaher *baritone*
Gerold Huber *piano*

'What bliss to write song!' Schumann's declaration to his beloved Clara resounds through all his Lieder, and nowhere more movingly than in *Dichterliebe*, his cycle about the joys and sorrows of love *(see panel, right)*.

Christian Gerhaher

Touching the very heart of Schumann's turbulent emotional world is a young German baritone with an international reputation as one of the major Lieder interpreters of our time.

There will be no interval

🔊 **2.15pm The Adverb** (CH)
See page 107

FOCUS ON … PCM 4
SCHUMANN THE SONGSMITH

On the 150th anniversary of his death, **Hilary Finch** celebrates the lyric art of a composer for whom song was the very stuff of life

'Lord, let not any man be mad. I, too, am just a poor wretch of a musician.' So spoke that itinerant fiddler, 'Der Spielmann', from Schumann's Op. 40 Hans Christian Andersen settings. These touching character vignettes – a quite new challenge to Schumann at the time – cast their own oblique and poignant light on a musician who not only composed songs but who, uniquely, lived in and through the medium of song. One of Schumann's earliest compositions was his response to the words of Shakespeare's Feste, 'Hey, ho, the wind and the rain'; and his last setting (from the *Maria Stuart* group) was an agonised lament and prayer for release. It immediately preceded the composer's own suicide attempt and eventual death in an asylum.

The much-reviled practice of following parallel tracks between life and work is entirely justified in Schumann's case. His 1840 cycle *Dichterliebe* ('Poet's Love') tells the story of his estrangement from his beloved Clara – and, in the reburgeoning within the final piano postlude, his reunion with her in May's eternal spring. The irony and bitterness so characteristic of Heine's poetry is very much there in the music, too, for those with ears to hear. And only the most perverse commentator could fail to grasp Schumann's empathy, if not identification, with Goethe's crazed artist-wanderer, the Harper, in the Op. 98a settings of songs from *Wilhelm Meister*. The harmony itself is in turmoil, the structure of the songs almost cracking under the strain of a disturbed psyche.

But Schumann's song-writing is not *merely* autobiographical. Its highly instinctive melodic inflections and rhythmic shaping give voice to the pulse, the breathing, the heartbeat of everyman. The physical demands it makes on a singer correspond to – indeed, incarnate – the soul-state of any particular song, from the barely articulated tear-filled dreams of *Dichterliebe* to the crazed brutality of the late *Husarenlieder*. In Schumann, the music itself becomes the emotional experience it expresses.

RIGHT
Robert and Clara Schumann: engraving by Friedrich Schauer

Every Prom live on BBC Radio 3 and bbc.co.uk/proms • Advance Booking from 15 May • General Booking from 12 June: 020 7589 8212

111

FOCUS ON … PCM 6
MARIN MARAIS

Edward Blakeman on a star musician at the Sun King's court

When Marin Marais was born 350 years ago, the sun was just rising on one of the most glorious eras of French music. The young Prince Louis had heralded it when he danced the role of Apollo in a court ballet, and on acceding to the throne he became the kingly embodiment of the god of the sun and music. Under Louis XIV – *le Roi soleil* – all the arts flourished, and music in particular became central to every aspect of life at the Palace of Versailles.

The musical style encouraged by Louis was distinctly French. Inspired by dance and the human voice, it was by turns flamboyantly rhetorical and affectingly eloquent. Lully was the dominant musical genius of the age, and his example directly influenced all the other composers gathered around him, among them Marais, who began his career playing bass viol in Lully's opera orchestra.

Marais was immortalised some years ago in the film *Tous les matins du monde*, which related his uneasy relationship with his teacher Sainte-Colombe – a reclusive man who practised the viol hidden away in a tree-house and who sent Marais packing when he discovered him eavesdropping beneath it! Sainte-Colombe further disapproved of Marais's rise to fame at court, but his contemporaries were unstinting in their admiration: 'Marais quite simply perfected the viol to the highest degree possible, and he was the first to reveal its full range and beauty in the many excellent pieces he wrote for it, and by the admirable way in which he played them.' 350 years later the legacy of that artistry is undiminished.

ABOVE
Marin Marais: portrait
by André Bouys, c1700

LEFT
Gérard Depardieu as Marais
in Alain Corneau's 1991
film *Tous les matins du monde*

PCM 5
1.00pm – c2.00pm

György Kurtág
Hommage à R. Sch.   10'

Schumann
Selected piano works   10'

Ian Wilson
red over black   c13'
BBC co-commission with the Royal
Philharmonic Society: world premiere

Mozart
Trio in E flat major, K498 'Kegelstatt'   20'

Martin Fröst *clarinet*
Pierre Lénert *viola*
Cédric Tiberghien *piano*

The combination of clarinet, viola and piano, invented by Mozart, inspired him to write one of his most original and mellifluous chamber works, and threw down the gauntlet to composers ever since. Ian Wilson is the most recent to take up the challenge in a work commissioned jointly by the Royal Philharmonic Society and BBC Radio 3 for the New Generation Artists. Anniversary composer Kurtág's tribute to Schumann is characteristically elusive: the distillation of dreams.

There will be no interval

🔊 **2.15pm The Adverb** (CH)
See page 107

PCM 6
1.00pm – c2.00pm

Marais
Pièces en trio – selections   20'
Pièces de viole, Book 2 – selections   8'

Anne Danican Philidor
Recorder Sonata in D minor   6'

La Barre
Pièces en trio, Book 1 – selections   10'

Lully
Le sommeil d'Atys   8'

La Simphonie du Marais
Hugo Reyne *flute/director*
François Nicolet *flute*
Anne-Marie Lasla *treble viol*
Catherine Arnoux *treble viol*
Emmanuelle Guigues *bass viol*
Marc Wolff *theorbo*

A Proms debut for chamber players from one of France's foremost early music ensembles. Dedicated to reviving the music of Lully and his contemporaries – they mount a new production of a Lully opera each year at the Vendée Festival – here they lift the curtain on the intimate world of music devised for Louis XIV's private entertainment, and in particular celebrate the anniversary of that genius of the viol, Marin Marais (see panel, left).

There will be no interval

🔊 **2.15pm The Adverb** (CH)
See page 107

Every Prom live on BBC Radio 3 and bbc.co.uk/proms • Advance Booking from 15 May • General Booking from 12 June: 020 7589 8212

more than skin deep...

The Gel is a unique blend of cesium salts and homoeopathics. We based the Gel on research by a surgeon practising western medicine in China. He discovered that the power of acupuncture lay in the activation of the enzyme acetylcholinesterase. He then created formulations that achieved the same effect without needles. These methods proved to be effective for relieving pain and treating a range of conditions including cuts, burns and skin problems. The Gel is ideal for daily skin rejuvenation or use on specific problem areas.

To buy the Gel call
020 7224 2332
£24+p&p
60ml jar

the Gel™

a mineral and homoeopathic blend that energizes and rejuvenates the **skin** at a deep level

Gagnon Essentials

"The Gel always feels cool on the face and I love putting it on. Better still, I love what it does for my skin."
Clare Maxwell-Hudson

"I walked headlong into a tree, scraping most of the skin off my thumb. I smeared the magic Gel on. The following day there was barely any trace of the wound."
Nona Summers writing in Vogue UK

"The Gel is the best kept skin-care secret in the beauty world."
Leslie Kenton

how the Gel works

The Gel **1** triggers acetylcholinesterase activity which **2** acts on the neurotransmitter acetylcholine to stimulate the nervous system in the area of application and **3** promote rejuvenation at a molecular level.

The Gel is made with care using pure, natural ingredients: Deionized water, cesium salts, hypericum, arnica, calendula, rhus tox, ledum, apis, ruta, sulphur, carbomer.

www.gagnontherapies.com

Gagnon Essentials from Gagnon Therapies Ltd, London W1U 1PY, UK. For external use only. If pregnant or breast-feeding consult your doctor before use. Do not use if sensitive to any of the ingredients.

....Is always recomended by Chelsea Smile

To keep in tune.....

Chelsea Smile
The Chelsea Dental Practice

WE ARE CURRENTLY INVITING NEW PATIENTS TO
JOIN OUR STATE OF THE ART DENTAL PRACTICE;
WE OFFER

- 1 hour teeth whitening
- Cerec crown and veneers inlays (one visit - no impressions)
- Implants
- Specialist Orthodontist - currently no waiting list
- Hygeinist/ Gum disease treatments
- Digital X-rays (up to 90% reduction in radiation)
- Botox and filler injections by leading Harley St clinician
- Free examination for children under 16 of existing patients
- Extensive out of hours emergency service
- Appointments available from 8am til 11pm weekdays
  and Saturdays
- Anti-snoring devices/sleep apnoea clinic
- Nervous patient programme
- INTEREST FREE CREDIT FACILITY FOR UP TO £25000
- RAPIDLY INCREASING AMERICAN PATIENT LIST

WE LOOK FORWARD TO HEARING FROM YOU

For more information or to book an appointment
call Sue on **020 7351 2298**
or visit our website at **www.chelseasmile.co.uk**

DR RICHARD POLLOCK B.D.S

THE CHELSEA DENTAL PRACTICE
57 MARKHAM ST
CHELSEA
LONDON
SW3 3NR

Chelsea Smile

Music to your ears...

the daily dawn chorus... the buzz of insect wings...
the cries, croaks and calls of nature that are all around you.

**Find out more about the UK's urban wildlife
with this FREE full colour guide from the RSPB**

WILDLIFE ON YOUR
DOORSTEP
Get closer to the wildlife around you

Call 0870 240 1001 and quote 'prom06'
Lines are open 9 am - 5 pm, Monday to Friday

Offer ends December 2006. Calls are charged at national rate. RSPB terms and conditions apply. Registered charity no 207076

Ray Kennedy (rspb-images.com)

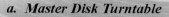

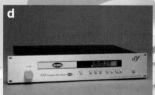

MOZART AT THE MOVIES AND SHOSTAKOVICH ON SCREEN

Royal Geographical Society, Kensington Gore
(entrance on Exhibition Road)
Admission free and unticketed *(limited capacity)*; doors open at 1.30pm.

Saturday 22 July 2.00pm – c4.30pm

PROMS FILM 1
The Magic Flute

Arguably one of the finest screen versions of an opera ever produced, Ingmar Bergman's 1975 film features leading Nordic singers of the day and a soundtrack recorded by the Swedish Radio Symphony Orchestra under Eric Ericson. Filming in a mock-up of the 18th-century Drottningholm Court Theatre, Bergman uses the full resources of the cinema to create a richly layered production that combines the best of screen and stage.
(Sung in Swedish with English subtitles; 135 mins; colour; certificate U)

Introduced by Simon Keefe, editor of *The Cambridge Companion to Mozart*

Sunday 30 July 2.00pm – c5.15pm

PROMS FILM 2
Amadeus (Director's cut)

A glorious celebration of the music of Mozart, Milos Forman's 1984 screen adaptation of Peter Shaffer's stage-play about the deadly rivalry between the jealous mediocrity Antonio Salieri and the divinely inspired Mozart went on to win eight Academy Awards. With music performed by the Academy of St Martin in the Fields under Sir Neville Marriner, the 'director's cut' includes 20 minutes of extra footage.
(173 mins; colour; certificate PG)

Introduced by Nicholas Kenyon, Director of the Proms and author of *The Faber Pocket Guide to Mozart*

Saturday 12 August
2.00pm – c4.45pm

PROMS FILM 3
Testimony

Based loosely on Dmitry Shostakovich's much-disputed 'memoirs', Tony Palmer's 1988 award-winning black-and-white film stars Ben Kingsley as the composer who somehow survived in the Soviet Union while countless other Russians perished every day. The music is performed by the London Philharmonic Orchestra, conducted by Rudolf Barshai.
(151 mins; b&w/colour; certificate PG)

Introduced by Tony Palmer, director of *Testimony*

Sunday 20 August 2.00pm – c4.30pm

PROMS FILM 4
Hamlet

The year after Stalin's death, the Russian director Grigori Kozintsev produced *Hamlet* on the stage. A decade later, in 1963, came his classic film. His colleague of 40 years, Dmitry Shostakovich, was persuaded to come out of 'retirement' as a film composer to write a score at the very peak of his form. The result is a stunning masterpiece: a triumph of controlled passion.
(In Russian with English subtitles; 140 mins; b&w; certificate U)

Introduced by Sam West, the Royal Shakespeare Company's *Hamlet* in 2001/2 and currently Artistic Director of Sheffield Theatres
(subject to availability)

ENHANCE YOUR PROMS EXPERIENCE

Every Prom broadcast live
Listen Again online (for seven days after broadcast)

Also listen out for

Sean Rafferty

Petroc Trelawny

In Tune – weekdays at 5.00pm
Sean Rafferty and Petroc Trelawny talking to all the
major performers and running weekly competitions

Penny Gore

Sandy Burnett

Martin Handley

Morning on 3 – every day at 7.00am
Penny Gore, Sandy Burnett, Martin Handley
and Sarah Walker presenting music and
updates on the season

Stephanie Hughes

Fiona Talkington

Sarah Walker

Talking Proms – weekly during Proms intervals
Stephanie Hughes, Fiona Talkington
and Sarah Walker with news
and background features

Ian McMillan

The Adverb – weekly during Proms intervals
With Ian McMillan and guest presenters.
Poetry and prose in performance,
recorded before a live audience
at Cadogan Hall immediately after
Proms Chamber Music concerts

**Get ready for the season
with Proms Preview Evening
on Thursday 13 July**

And more
Summer CD Review
Proms Sunday Features
Proms Composer Portraits

BBC RADIO 3*

90-93 FM

bbc.co.uk/radio3

THE BBC PROMS – MORE WAYS TO TUNE IN

The BBC: bringing the Proms to you – not just in concert,
but on radio, television, online and on your mobile phone as well

bbc.co.uk/proms

Listening to the Proms on DAB Digital Radio, online and via Digital TV (Satellite, Cable and Freeview)

Not only can you listen to every Prom in digital sound
via BBC Radio 3
but you can also receive concert information during
each broadcast while you listen (*on DAB Digital Radio,
online and Freeview*)

Watching the Proms on Digital TV (Satellite, Cable and Freeview)

Not only can you watch the best of the Proms season in both
live and deferred relays on BBC ONE, BBC TWO and BBC FOUR
but you can also access specially-written programme notes
or synchronised captions by pressing red on your digital remote.
Plus, on the Last Night, press red to see the notes and choose
a Proms in the Park concert from around the UK

Interacting with the Proms online

Not only can you get full concert information on the BBC Proms website at bbc.co.uk/proms **but you can also** book tickets online via the Royal Albert Hall website

Not only can you listen live to every Prom via the website **but you can also** listen again to most Proms for seven days after broadcast

Not only can you take part in a wide range of Proms debates on our messageboard **but you could also** win tickets by sending in your reviews of Proms concerts

Keeping in touch with the Proms on your mobile phone

Not only can you sign up for free daily text updates during the Proms season (text PROMS CLUB to 83111*) **but you can also** access full Proms listings and broadcast information at any time via the Proms mobile site at bbc.co.uk/mobile**

* You will be charged your usual text rates for registration to the service. Each message you receive will be free to you. To unsubscribe at any time text STOP to 83111. Full terms and conditions available on the Proms website – bbc.co.uk/proms
**WAP-enabled phones only

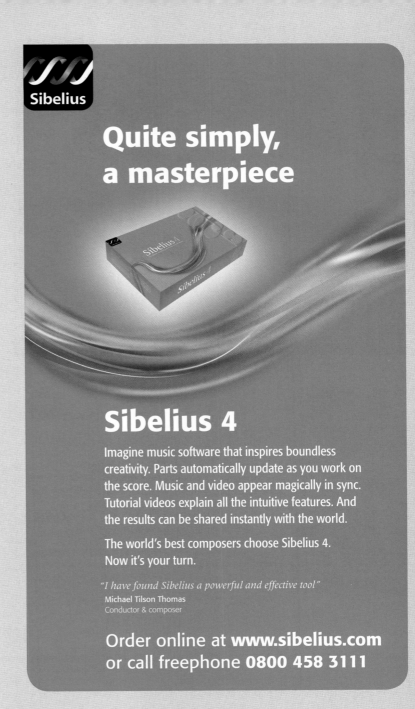

ST GEORGE'S CHAPEL CHOIR, WINDSOR CASTLE

The Choir of St George's Chapel, Windsor Castle, has been in existence since 1348 and, with the exception of the Civil War, has sung services in the Chapel continuously since then. Its 18 boy choristers and 12 lay clerks have also provided the music for many ceremonies of royal and national significance, including the annual Thanksgiving Service of the Order of the Garter, the Service of Prayer and Dedication on the Marriage of Their Royal Highnesses The Prince of Wales and The Duchess of Cornwall, and the 80th birthday celebrations of Her Majesty The Queen. In recent years the Choir has extended its boundaries beyond the daily worship in the Chapel through concerts, most recently at the Barbican, recordings on the Naxos and Delphian labels, and foreign tours.

Tim Byram-Wigfield, Director of Music, is pleased to receive enquiries
from prospective choristers, lay clerks, deputies and organ scholars at any time.

To find out more about life as chorister, come along to our
Chorister Open Day on Saturday 7th October 2006 and attend the
Chorister Auditions on Saturday 4th November 2006.

Please contact Francesca Russill, Secretary to the Director of Music,
8c The Cloisters, Windsor Castle, Berkshire SL4 1NJ.
Tel: 01753 848797 • Email: music@stgeorges-windsor.org

HOW TO BOOK

ADVANCE BOOKING
By post, fax and online – opens Monday 15 May

Use the Advance Booking Form or visit bbc.co.uk/proms

To take advantage of the Advance Booking period – and enjoy your best chance of securing the seats you want – you must use the official Advance Booking Form (facing page 142) or the Online Ticket Request system on the Proms website.

Note that all postal, fax and online bookings received before Monday 15 May will be treated as if they had arrived on that date and that Express Bookings will then be handled first (for full details see page 141).

Postal address: BBC Proms, Box Office,
Royal Albert Hall, London SW7 2AP
Fax: 020 7581 9311
Online booking: bbc.co.uk/proms

For Concert Listings, see pages 59–113

GENERAL BOOKING
In person, by phone or online – opens Monday 12 June

The Royal Albert Hall Box Office is located at Door 12 and is open 9.00am–9.00pm daily. Note that no booking fee applies to tickets bought in person at the Hall.

Telephone: 020 7589 8212
Online booking: bbc.co.uk/proms

THE LAST NIGHT OF THE PROMS

Because of the high demand for tickets, special booking arrangements apply. For full details – and your chance to enter the Last Night Ballot (exclusive to readers of the *BBC Proms 2006 Guide*) – see page 139.

PROMMING ON THE DAY – Don't book, just turn up

Up to 1,400 standing places are available for each concert at the Royal Albert Hall. Weekend Promming Passes and Season Tickets can be booked in advance: see pages 134 and 135. Additionally, over 500 Arena and Gallery tickets are always on sale at the door from an hour beforehand, so you can just turn up on the night.

PROMS AT CADOGAN HALL

For booking information on the Proms Saturday Matinee and Proms Chamber Music series, see page 107.

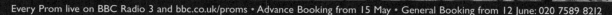
Every Prom live on BBC Radio 3 and bbc.co.uk/proms • Advance Booking from 15 May • General Booking from 12 June: 020 7589 8212

HOW TO PROM AT THE ROYAL ALBERT HALL

What is Promming?

The popular tradition of Promming is central to the unique and informal atmosphere of the BBC Proms at the Royal Albert Hall.

Up to 1,400 standing places are available at each Proms concert. The traditionally low prices allow you to enjoy world-class concerts for just £5.00 each (or even less with a Season Ticket or Weekend Promming Pass). There are two standing areas: the Arena, located directly in front of the stage, and the Gallery, running round the top of the Hall. All spaces are unreserved.

Day Prommers

Over 500 Arena and Gallery tickets (priced £5.00) go on sale on the day 30 minutes before doors open (one hour before on days when there are Pre-Prom Talks). These tickets cannot be booked in advance, so even if all seats have been sold, you always have a good chance of getting in (though early queuing is advisable for the more popular concerts). You must buy your ticket in person, and can pay in cash only.

Wheelchair-users who wish to Prom (Gallery only) should queue in the same way but will be redirected to Door 8 once their ticket is purchased. (For further information for disabled concert-goers, see page 138.)

Day tickets are available (for cash only) at Door 11 (Arena) and Door 10 (Gallery), not at the Box Office. If in doubt about where to go, Royal Albert Hall stewards will point you in the right direction.

Over 500 Arena and Gallery tickets (priced at £5.00) go on sale on the day 30 minutes before doors open.

Prommers' Season Tickets

Frequent Prommers can save money by purchasing Arena or Gallery Season Tickets covering either the whole Proms season (including the Last Night) or only the first or second half (ie Proms 1–37 or Proms 36–72, excluding the Last Night).

Season Ticket-holders benefit from:
- guaranteed entrance (until 10 minutes before each concert)
- great savings – prices can work out at less than £2.00 per concert
- guaranteed entrance to the Last Night for Whole Season Ticket-holders and special access to a reserved allocation of Last Night tickets for Half Season Ticket-holders. See page 139.

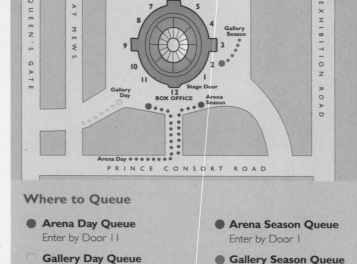

Where to Queue

- **Arena Day Queue**
  Enter by Door 11

- **Gallery Day Queue**
  Enter by Door 10

- **Arena Season Queue**
  Enter by Door 1

- **Gallery Season Queue**
  Enter by Door 2

Please note that Season Ticket-holders arriving at the Hall later than 10 minutes before a concert are not guaranteed entry and may be asked, in certain circumstances, to join the day queue.

Please note that Season Tickets are non-transferable; two passport-sized photographs must be provided before tickets can be issued.

For further details and prices of Season Tickets, see page 141.

For further details and prices of Weekend Promming Passes, see facing page.

Proms at Cadogan Hall

For Cadogan Hall booking information, see page 107.

Every Prom live on BBC Radio 3 and bbc.co.uk/proms • Advance Booking from 15 May • General Booking from 12 June: 020 7589 8212

134

Same Day Savers

Book for more than one concert on the same day and save £4.00 on your ticket for each subsequent concert.

Note: offer applies to matinee, evening and late-night performances in the Royal Albert Hall only. Not valid for Arena, Gallery and Circle (Restricted View) price areas.

Under-16s

The Proms are a great way to discover live music, and we encourage anyone over 5 years old to attend. Tickets for under-16s can be purchased at half-price in any seating area for all Proms except the Last Night (Prom 73).

Note that the Blue Peter Proms (Proms 10 & 12) are expressly designed to introduce young children to concert-going.

Group Bookings

Group booking rates apply to all Proms except the Last Night (Prom 73). Groups of 10 or more can claim a 10% discount (5% for C band concerts) on the price of Centre/Side Stalls or Front/Rear Circle tickets.

For more information, call the Group Booking Information Line: 020 7838 3108.

Please note that group purchases cannot be made online during the General Booking period.

Groups of 10 or more can claim a 10% discount

Weekend Promming Pass

Beat the queues at the weekend and save money! In addition to discounted tickets, the Weekend Promming Pass offers guaranteed access up to 10 minutes before start-time to the Arena or Gallery standing areas for all concerts in the Royal Albert Hall on Fridays, Saturdays and Sundays (excluding Proms 10, 12, 72 and 73). Passes can be purchased in advance, by post or fax (using the Advance Booking Form) or online, and (from Monday 12 June) by phone or in person at the Box Office up to 6.00pm on Friday nights (5.30pm on 4 August). Prices vary for each weekend depending on the number of concerts covered.

Note that Weekend 2 excludes the Blue Peter Proms (10 & 12); Weekend 7 includes Bank Holiday Monday (28 August); and there is no pass covering Proms 72 and 73.

Passes are non-transferable and signature ID may be requested upon entry. Purchase of a Weekend Pass does not guarantee entry to the Last Night, but tickets may be counted towards the 'Six Concert Rule' (see page 139) in conjunction with further Passes or Day Ticket stubs.

Note that you may only purchase a maximum of four passes per weekend (subject to availability).

For whole and half-season Season Tickets, see facing page.

Weekend Promming Pass prices		
Weekend 1	Proms 1–3	£12.50
Weekend 2	Proms 9, 11 & 13	£12.50
Weekend 3	Proms 19–22	£17.50
Weekend 4	Proms 28–32	£22.50
Weekend 5	Proms 38–41	£17.50
Weekend 6	Proms 47–49	£12.50
Weekend 7	Proms 55–59	£22.50
Weekend 8	Proms 64–66	£12.50

Every Prom live on BBC Radio 3 and bbc.co.uk/proms • Advance Booking from 15 May • General Booking from 12 June: 020 7589 8212

135

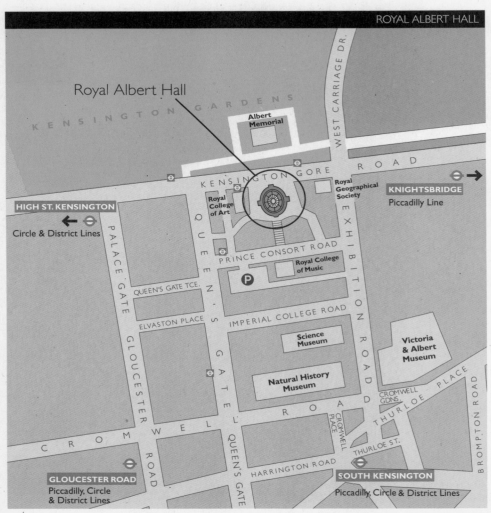

ROYAL ALBERT HALL

Royal Albert Hall

Albert Memorial

KENSINGTON GARDENS

WEST CARRIAGE DR.

KENSINGTON GORE ROAD

HIGH ST. KENSINGTON
← Circle & District Lines

Royal College of Art

Royal Geographical Society

KNIGHTSBRIDGE
Piccadilly Line →

PRINCE CONSORT ROAD

Royal College of Music

QUEEN'S GATE TCE.

QUEEN'S GATE

PALACE GATE

GLOUCESTER ROAD

ELVASTON PLACE

IMPERIAL COLLEGE ROAD

EXHIBITION ROAD

Science Museum

Victoria & Albert Museum

Natural History Museum

CROMWELL ROAD

CROMWELL GDNS.

CROMWELL PLACE

THURLOE PLACE

BROMPTON ROAD

THURLOE ST.

GLOUCESTER ROAD
Piccadilly, Circle & District Lines

HARRINGTON ROAD

SOUTH KENSINGTON
Piccadilly, Circle & District Lines

The following buses serve the Royal Albert Hall (via Kensington Gore, Queen's Gate and/or Prince Consort Road): Nos. 9/N9, 10/N10, 52/N52, 70, 360

The following buses serve Cadogan Hall (via Sloane Street and/or Sloane Square): Nos. 11, 19, 22, 137, 139, 211, 319, 360, C1

For 24-hour London Travel Information, call 020 7222 1234 or visit www.tfl.gov.uk

Note that both the Royal Albert Hall and Cadogan Hall lie outside the Congestion Charging Zone. For car parking at the Royal Albert Hall, see facing page.

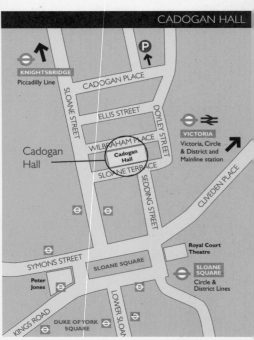

CADOGAN HALL

KNIGHTSBRIDGE
Piccadilly Line

CADOGAN PLACE

SLOANE STREET

ELLIS STREET

DOVLEY STREET

VICTORIA
Victoria, Circle & District and Mainline station →

Cadogan Hall

WILBRAHAM PLACE

Cadogan Hall

SLOANE TERRACE

SEDDING STREET

CLIVEDEN PLACE

Royal Court Theatre

SYMONS STREET

SLOANE SQUARE

SLOANE SQUARE
Circle & District Lines

Peter Jones

KINGS ROAD

DUKE OF YORK SQUARE

LOWER SLOAN

Every Prom live on BBC Radio 3 and bbc.co.uk/proms • Advance Booking from 15 May • General Booking from 12 June: 020 7589 8212

136

Restaurants The Royal Albert Hall offers a choice of three restaurants.

The Elgar Restaurant offers a fine dining experience with full table service. Enter via Door 8 to Circle level.

The Victoria Restaurant offers an Italian menu of light starters, pizza and pasta. Enter via Door 1 to Circle level.

The Café Consort offers a full menu, including salads, sandwiches and light meals. It is also open in the daytime, offering coffee and a selection of light meals, as well as for meals after the concert on selected dates (call 020 7589 8212 for details). Enter via Door 12.

The Victoria and Elgar Restaurants open two hours before the performance start-time; the Café Consort opens two and a half hours before the start-time.

All restaurants can be booked in advance. Call 020 7589 8212 to make a reservation or visit www.royalalberthall.com for more information.

Bars
The Champagne and North Circle bars, offering a range of sandwiches and snacks, open two hours before the start of the performance. All other bars open 45 minutes before the start of the performance.

Catering in your box
Offering sandwiches, a two-course supper with a full range of beverages or simply interval drinks, hospitality can be pre-ordered by telephoning 020 7589 5666. Please allow two working days' notice.

Please note that you are not permitted to consume your own food and drink inside the Hall. For safety reasons, glasses and bottles are not allowed in the auditorium except as part of box hospitality ordered through the Hall's caterers.

Car Parking
A limited number of parking spaces are available from 6.00pm in the Imperial College Car Park (Prince Consort or Exhibition Road entrances). These can be booked in advance (priced £7.50) using the Advance Booking Form (facing page 142), online (from 12 June) or by telephoning the Box Office on 020 7589 8212, 9.00am–9.00pm daily (from 12 June). Please note that, if attending both early-evening and late-night concerts, only one parking fee is payable.

The Café Consort offers a full menu, including salads, sandwiches and light meals

Ticket collection kiosks are now available within the Box Office at Door 12.

Doors open 45 minutes before each concert (earlier for restaurant and bar access).

Latecomers will not be admitted into the auditorium unless or until there is a suitable break in the music. There is a video monitor with digital audio relay in the foyer at Door 6.

Bags and coats may be left in the cloakrooms at Door 9 (ground level) and at basement level beneath Door 6. Folding chairs and hand-luggage larger than a briefcase are not allowed in the auditorium.

Security In the interests of audience safety, bags may be searched upon entry.

Children under 5 Out of consideration for both audience and artists, children under the age of 5 are not allowed in the auditorium.

Dress Code There is no dress code at the Proms.

Mobile phones and watch alarms should be turned off.

The use of cameras, video cameras and recording equipment is strictly forbidden.

Smoking is permitted in the following areas only: North Circle Bar; bars and foyers at Door 3 (including the ground-floor foyer but excluding the East Porch bar); West Arena Bar. Smoking is banned in all other areas.

Tours of the Royal Albert Hall
Tours run daily (except Wednesdays and Thursdays) and last around 45 minutes. Telephone 020 7838 3105 for further information and to check times. Ticket prices range from £4.00 to £7.50 with a number of concessions available.

Royal Albert Hall Shop
The Royal Albert Hall Shop, offering a selection of Proms and Royal Albert Hall gifts and souvenirs, is located in the South Porch at Door 12. The Shop is open daily from 10.00am to 6.00pm. Proms merchandise can also be purchased at Door 6 Foyer during performance times.

Every Prom live on BBC Radio 3 and bbc.co.uk/proms • Advance Booking from 15 May • General Booking from 12 June: 020 7589 8212

137

INFORMATION FOR DISABLED CONCERT-GOERS

Access at the Proms

Call the Access Information Line on 020 7838 3110 for advice on facilities for disabled concert-goers (including car parking) at all Proms venues; if you have any special requirements; or to request a Royal Albert Hall Access leaflet. Dedicated staff will be available daily from 9.00am to 9.00pm. The Access leaflet is also available from the Hall's website: www.royalalberthall.com.

Wheelchair access

 Wheelchair access is available at all Proms venues, but advance booking is advised.

Royal Albert Hall

The Royal Albert Hall has up to 14 spaces bookable in the Stalls for wheelchair-users and their companions (entrance via Door 8). End-of-aisle places are priced as Centre Stalls seats; front-row platform places either side of the stage are priced as Side Stalls seats; rear platform places are priced as Front Circle seats. There are up to six spaces in the Front Circle, priced as such. When filling in the Booking Form, tick your preferred price range (ie Centre Stalls, Side Stalls or Front Circle) and enter the number of places required under the 'Wheelchair space' column.

Four wheelchair spaces are available in the Gallery for Promming. These cannot be pre-booked. (See page 134 for 'How to Prom' at the Royal Albert Hall'.)

Passenger lifts at the Royal Albert Hall are located on the ground-floor corridor at Doors 1 and 8. Use of lifts is discouraged during performances.

Cadogan Hall

Cadogan Hall has a range of services to assist disabled customers, including a provision for wheelchair-users in the Stalls. There are three wheelchair spaces available for advance booking and one space reserved for sale from 10.00am on the day of the concert.
For information, call 020 7730 4500.

Discounts for disabled concert-goers

Disabled concert-goers (and one companion) receive a 50% discount on all ticket prices (except Arena and Gallery areas) for concerts at the Royal Albert Hall and for Proms Matinee and Chamber Music concerts at Cadogan Hall. To claim this discount, tick the box on Part 3 of the Booking

Visually-impaired patrons are welcome to use the free infra-red hearing facility to listen in to the broadcast commentary on Radio 3

Form, or call the Access Information Line on 020 7838 3110 if booking by phone (from Monday 12 June). Note that discounts for disabled concert-goers cannot be combined with other ticket offers.

Tickets can also be purchased in person from Monday 12 June at the Royal Albert Hall. The Box Office is situated at Door 12 and has ramped access, an induction loop and drop-down counters.

 The Royal Albert Hall has an infra-red system with a number of personal receivers for use with and without hearing aids. To make use of the service, collect a free receiver from the Door 6 Information Desk.

If you have a guide dog, the best place to sit in the Royal Albert Hall is in a Loggia or Second Tier Box, where your dog may stay with you. If you are sitting elsewhere, stewards will be happy to look after your dog while you enjoy the concert. Please call the Access Information Line on 020 7838 3110 to organise in advance of your visit.

Proms Guide: non-print versions

Audio cassette, CD, braille and computer disk versions of this Guide are available in two parts, 'Articles' and 'Concert Listings/Booking Information', priced £2.50 each or £5.00 for both. For more information and to order, contact RNIB Customer Services: 0845 7023 153.

Radio 3 commentary

Visually-impaired patrons are welcome to use the free infra-red hearing facility (see above) to listen in to the broadcast commentary on Radio 3.

Programme-reading service

Ask at the Door 6 Information Desk if you would like a steward to read your concert programme out to you.

Large-print programmes & texts

Large-print concert programmes can be made available on the night (at the same price as the standard programme) if ordered not less than five working days in advance. Complimentary large-print texts and opera librettos (where applicable) can also be made available on the night if ordered in advance. To order any large-print programmes or texts, please telephone 020 7765 3260. They will be left for collection at the Door 6 Information Desk 45 minutes before the start of the concert.

Every Prom live on BBC Radio 3 and bbc.co.uk/proms • Advance Booking from 15 May • General Booking from 12 June: 020 7589 8212

138

PRICE BANDS FOR PROMS IN THE ROYAL ALBERT HALL

Seats

Each concert falls into one of seven different price bands, colour-coded for easy reference

	A	B	C	D	E	F	G
Centre Stalls	£24.00	£32.00	£40.00	£12.50	£15.00	£73.00	
Side Stalls	£22.00	£29.00	£37.00	£12.50	£15.00	£70.00	
Loggia Boxes (8 seats)	£27.00	£34.00	£42.00	£12.50	£15.00	£75.00	
2nd Tier Boxes (5 seats)	£18.00	£23.00	£33.00	£12.50	£15.00	£70.00	ALL SEATS £10.00 (UNDER-16s £5.00)
Choir	£15.00	£18.00	£25.00	N/A	N/A	£52.50	
Front Circle	£13.00	£16.00	£20.00	£9.00	£12.50	£52.50	
Rear Circle	£10.00	£11.00	£14.50	£9.00	£12.50	£40.00	
Circle (restricted view)	£6.00	£7.00	£10.00	N/A	N/A	£20.00	

Promming

Standing places are available in the Arena and Gallery on the day for £5.00 (see page 134)

Season Tickets	**Dates**	**Arena**	**Gallery**
Whole Season (Proms 1–73)	14 July – 9 September	**£160.00**	**£135.00**
Half Season tickets			
First Half (Proms 1–37)	14 July – 10 August	**£90.00**	**£75.00**
Second Half (Proms 36–72)	10 August – 8 September	**£90.00**	**£75.00**

BBC Proms in the Park, London, Saturday 9 September

All tickets £23.00 (for further details of this and other Proms in the Park venues, see pages 103–105)

Please note that booking fees apply to all postal, fax, telephone and online bookings (for details, see Booking Form).

Unwanted tickets may be exchanged for tickets to other Proms concerts (subject to availability). A fee of £1.00 per ticket will be charged for this service. Telephone the Royal Albert Hall Box Office (020 7589 8212) for further details.

Express Bookings
All booking forms that include a request for an A band concert qualify for Express Booking. To increase your chances of getting the tickets you want for the more popular concerts in price bands B and C, you are advised to book for at least one A band concert as well.
NB: If you are only booking for one of the two Blue Peter Proms (price band G), your booking will also qualify for fast-tracking. Tick the box at the end of the Booking Form if you think your application qualifies.

Disabled Concert-goers
See page 138 for details of special discounts, access and facilities.

Privately-owned Seats
A high proportion of boxes, as well as 650 Stalls seats, are privately owned. Unless returned by owners, these seats are not usually available for sale.

Season Tickets
Season Tickets and PCM Series Passes can be booked by post, fax or online from Monday 15 May and by phone or in person at the Box Office from Monday 12 June. For postal and fax bookings, complete the special section of the Booking Form (facing page 142). Please note that two passport-sized photographs must be provided for each ticket or pass before it can be issued.

Proms at Cadogan Hall
For booking information on the Proms Saturday Matinee and Proms Chamber Music series, see page 107.

Every Prom live on BBC Radio 3 and bbc.co.uk/proms • Advance Booking from 15 May • General Booking from 12 June: 020 7589 8212

141

HOW TO FILL IN THE ADVANCE BOOKING FORM

- **Choose the concerts** you want to go to and where you want to sit.

- **Enter the number of tickets** you require for each concert under your chosen seating area (adult tickets on the white squares, under-16s on the blue).

- **Add up the value of tickets** requested and enter the amount in the 'Sub-total' column.

- **If claiming any special offers** (see page 135) or disabled concert-goers' discounts (see page 138), enter the total value of discounts claimed for each concert in the red 'Discount' column. Then subtract the value of the discount from the 'Sub-total' and enter the 'Total' at the end of the row (adding in any Car Parking fee, if applicable).

- **If the tickets you request are not available**, you can opt to receive either lower-priced or higher-priced alternatives by ticking the appropriate box at the end of the Booking Form.

- **If booking by fax**, clearly enter your name at the top of all three pages and tick the box at the end of Part 3. Please do not duplicate your fax booking by post or online. Note that fax booking lines are open 24 hours a day.

Booking Queries

If you have any queries about how to fill in the Booking Form, call the Box Office on 020 7589 8212 (open 9.00am–9.00pm daily).

Online Booking

For details of how to book online, visit the BBC Proms website at bbc.co.uk/proms Note that, from this year, once general booking opens (on Monday 12 June), online customers will now be able to choose their own seats.

Check List

Before posting or faxing your booking form, please check that you have:

- [ ] Filled in your name at the top of all three pages.
- [ ] Indicated whether you will accept lower- or higher-priced tickets.
- [ ] Entered your data protection preferences.
- [ ] Enclosed two passport-sized photographs for each Proms Season Ticket or PCM Series Pass applied for.
- [ ] Sent back all three pages.

ADVANCE BOOKING FORM PART 1 — Full name of sender, Surname SHARPE, First Name DEE

ADVANCE BOOKING FORM PART 3 — Full name of sender, Surname SHARPE

BBC Proms in the Park, London, Saturday 9 September

For details of this and other Proms in the Park venues, see pages 103–105

	Number of tickets	Total (£)
All tickets: £23.00	6	Part 3 Total 139:00

	Parts 1&2 Total	Part 3 Total	Booking fee	
Sum of totals	£ 236:00	+ £ 139:00	+ £2.50 = Grand Total £ 376:00

(BLOCK CAPITALS PLEASE)

Title — First name — Surname

Address

Postcode

County — Evening telephone

Daytime telephone

lower-priced tickets / higher-priced tickets

I am booking by fax and will post two clearly-labelled p...

Every Prom live on BBC Radio 3 and bbc.co.uk/proms • Advance Booking from 15 May • General Booking from 12 June: 020 7589 8212

142

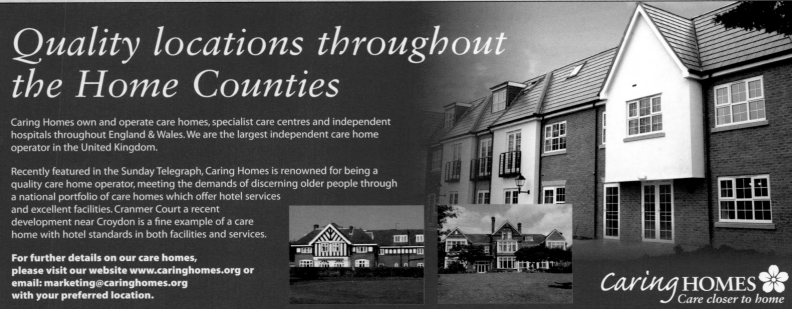

The Royal Society of Musicians of Great Britain

FOUNDED 1738 INCORPORATED BY ROYAL CHARTERS 1790 & 1987

The Royal Society of Musicians of Great Britain was founded by Handel and others to support professional musicians and their families when in distress because of illness, accident or old age. Its charitable work has continued, responding to increasing need and acting swiftly in cases of emergency.

If you know a musician needing help
please let us know at once.

If you wish to help us
please send us a donation or arrange for Gift Aid or GAYE donations or a legacy.

For details please contact: The Secretary
The Royal Society of Musicians of Great Britain
10 Stratford Place, London W1C 1BA
Telephone 020 7629 6137

Registered Charity Number 208879

THE National Children's Orchestra OF Great Britain

Auditions FOR 2007 to be held Autumn 2006

[Five age-banded Orchestras for talented children aged between 7 and 13]
[Some free places available through our bursary and scholarship schemes]

For more information and an audition application form please contact:

Administrative Secretary
The National Children's Orchestra
84a Elm Tree Road, Locking
Weston-super-Mare
Somerset BS24 8EH

Tel. 01934 820 254
Email. mail@nco.org.uk
Web. www.nco.org.uk

Future Performances 2006

Leeds Town Hall - 13th August
Main Orchestra - 3pm

Octagon Hall, Pavillion Gardens, Buxton - 2nd September
Under 13 Orchestra - 3pm

Queen Elizabeth Hall, London - 17th December
Under 13 Orchestra - 3pm - Main Orchestra - 7.30pm

Photograph by Ian Gillett

❖ YAMAHA   CLASSIC fM   The Leverhulme Trust   The Weston Family

PRESENTS

In partnership with

ŽIDOVSKÉ MUZEUM V PRAZE

INTERNATIONALES KAMMERMUSIKFESTIVAL NÜRNBERG

Music by **Jonathan Dove** and **Matthew King**
Libretto compiled by **Tertia Sefton-Green**

The world premiere of a compelling music theatre piece which gives voice to the words of children whose own voices were silenced – children of the Holocaust.

Featuring: Soprano Alison Buchanan, The Fürth Streichhölzer Youth Orchestra, Slavíčci Youth Choir and performers from London, Nuremberg and Prague. Conductor Peter Selwyn.

LONDON	NUREMBERG	PRAGUE
Sat 15 July 7.30pm	Tue 18 July 2006 7.30pm	Thu 20 July 2006 7.30pm
Sun 16 July 2.30pm	Fürth Stadttheater	Prague State Opera
UCL Bloomsbury Theatre	CALL Theater Kasse	CALL BTI
020 7388 8822	+49(0) 911 9 74 24 00	+42(0) 2242 27832 / 37727
www.thebloomsbury.com	www.stadttheater.fuerth.de	www.ticketsbti.cz
£15, £12.50 concs		

Hear Our Voice
WORLD PREMIERE TOUR 15 – 20 JULY 2006

Bloomsbury
the UCL theatre

PRSFoundation for new music

ARTS COUNCIL ENGLAND

Culture 2000

Fall in love with entertainment all over your home.

Living Control's luxury multi-room entertainment system places all your music, satellite, TV and video at your fingertips in any room.

No more wires, ugly boxes, CD or DVD racks, little décor-matching in-room touchscreens do all the work.

Select audio and video by name, integrate your iPod® and control lights, curtains and blinds whenever and wherever the mood takes you. Liberate your décor and living space and enjoy the best entertainment everywhere – even in the garden – with the luxury of fingertip control.

See this system in operation at our showroom in Poundbury, Dorchester. Alternatively to receive a brochure please call or email install@stoneaudio.co.uk

iPod® is a registered trademark of Apple Computer, Inc..

Living**Control**

Promise a safer future for Frazzle

LITTLE FRAZZLE was set on fire and left to die. Thanks to the RSPCA and its branches, he's safe in a new home now. Sadly though, his case isn't as rare as we would like – in just one year we investigated around 100,000 reports of animal cruelty. We work hard to protect defenceless animals, but we rely on the generosity of the kind people who remember us in their Wills to do so.

If you can leave a gift to the RSPCA, you'll leave the promise of a safer future for loving pets like Frazzle. Your gift will help us work long into the future to make a safer world for animals – and always be here for the victims of neglect and cruelty.

© Ross Parry

For a simple guide to making or changing your Will, return the coupon below or call, quoting reference number 06NL01 007 0

0870 9062 100

Lines are open 24 hours a day, 7 days a week

Part of the 'Remember A Charity' Campaign

Please tell me how my Will can help leave a safer future for animals.

Please send me information on: *(tick as appropriate)*

☐ Making a Will   ☐ Amending a Will

Name_____

Address_____

_____

_____ Postcode_____

06NL01 007 0

Please return this coupon to:
Joanna Curtis, RSPCA, FREEPOST SEA 10503, Horsham RH13 9BR

We receive no government funding

The RSPCA operates in England and Wales

RSPCA

Registered Charity no. 219099

Discover the Rhythm of Life

See Britain's most impressive display of musical instruments brought to life in a breathtaking gallery

'A world class gallery celebrating music'

Jools Holland,
Horniman Museum
Patron

HORNIMAN MUSEUM

100 London Road • Forest Hill • SE23
FREE admission • Tel 020 8699 1872

Free parking in surrounding streets
Train Forest Hill

Index of Artists

Bold italic figures refer to Prom numbers
(PSM indicates Proms Saturday Matinees: see pages 108–9.
PCM indicates Proms Chamber Music concerts: see pages 110–13)
* First appearance at a BBC Henry Wood Promenade Concert

Olga Sergeeva *soprano** 3
Gil Shaham *violin* 56
Alexander Shelley *conductor** 10, 12
Alexandra Sherman *mezzo-soprano** 22
Brindley Sherratt *bass* 2
Vassily Sinaisky *conductor* 23
Adrian Spillett *percussion** 37
Christianne Stotijn *mezzo-soprano** 70
Hilary Summers *mezzo-soprano* 33
Rowland Sutherland *piccolo** 37

Bryn Terfel *bass-baritone* 13
Christian Tetzlaff *violin* 43
Cédric Tiberghien *piano** PCM 5
Sir John Tomlinson *bass* 1
Yan Pascal Tortelier *conductor* 34
Ailish Tynan *soprano* 2

Dawn Upshaw *soprano* 54

Osmo Vänskä *conductor* 54
Maxim Vengerov *violin/conductor* 40
Roger Vignoles *piano* PCM 2
Volker Vogel *tenor* 3
Lars Vogt *piano* 59
Ilan Volkov *conductor* 35, 36
Anke Vondung *mezzo-soprano** 6

Sam Walton *percussion** 37
Richard Watkins *horn** 4
Jon Fredric West *tenor** 3
Roderick Williams *baritone* 24
Barry Wordsworth *conductor* 15

Manickam Yogeswaran *singer** 20

Z

Thomas Zehetmair *conductor/violin* 9
Qiu Lin Zhang *mezzo-soprano** 3
Frank Peter Zimmermann *violin* 65
Nikolaj Znaider *violin* 55

Groups

Academy of Ancient Music PSM 2
Bamberg Symphony Orchestra* 18
BBC Concert Orchestra 15, 58
BBC National Chorus of Wales 13
BBC National Orchestra of Wales 11, 13, 27, 69
BBC Philharmonic 8, 10, 12, 22, 23, 34
BBC Scottish Symphony Orchestra 19, 20, 35, 36
BBC Singers 2, 22, 52, 63, 73
BBC Symphony Chorus 1, 21, 32, 66, 70, 73
BBC Symphony Orchestra 1, 7, 14, 21, 26, 32, 38, 43, 52, 55, 62, 70, 73
Berliner Philharmoniker 64, 65
Britten Sinfonia PSM 3
Budapest Festival Orchestra 44
Camerata Salzburg 68
Children's International Voices of Enfield* 7
Choir of the Enlightenment 72
Choristers of the Chapels Royal, St James Palace & Hampton Court Palace* 7
City of Birmingham Symphony Orchestra 16
City of Birmingham Symphony Youth Chorus 7
Collegium Vocale Gent 57
Côr Caerdydd* 13
English Baroque Soloists 17
English Concert 24
English Concert, Choir of 24
European Union Youth Orchestra 39
Fanfare Trumpeters of the Scots Guards* 7
Finchley Children's Music Group 7
Finnish Radio Symphony Orchestra 42
Glyndebourne Chorus 6
Gustav Mahler Jugendorchester 51
Hallé 4
His Majestys Sagbutts & Cornetts 17
Huddersfield Choral Society 21
Islington Children's Music Group 10, 12
King's Consort 33
King's Consort, Choir of 33
Leopold String Trio PCM 7
London Brass 13
London Mozart Players PSM 1
London Philharmonic Choir 53
London Philharmonic Orchestra 53
London Sinfonietta 25
London Symphony Chorus 13, 70
London Symphony Orchestra 47, 50
London Winds 5
Mariinsky Theatre (Kirov Opera), Chorus and Orchestra of 48, 49
Minnesota Orchestra* 54
Monteverdi Choir 17
Nash Ensemble 63
National Youth Choir of Great Britain 20

National Youth Choir of Scotland* 20
National Youth Orchestra of Great Britain 30
NDR Symphony Orchestra 56
New London Children's Choir 7
Northern Sinfonia 9
Orchestra of St Luke's* 45
Orchestra of the Age of Enlightenment 6, 72
Orchestre de Paris 3
Orchestre des Champs-Élysées* 57
Orchestre National de France* 60
OSJ PSM 4
OSJ Voices* PSM 4
Philadelphia Orchestra 66, 67
Philharmonia Chorus 53
Philharmonia Orchestra 41
Pittsburgh Symphony Orchestra 61
Radio Tarifa* 29
Rodolfus Choir 20
Royal Philharmonic Orchestra 71
Royal Scottish National Orchestra 28
Royal String Quartet* PCM 3
Salzburg Mozarteum Orchestra* 59
Scottish Chamber Orchestra 2
Simphonie du Marais* PCM 6
Solistes de l'Orchestre de Paris* PCM 1
Southend Boys' & Girls' Choirs 7
Synergy Vocals* 37
The Shout* 20, 21
Trinity Boys' Choir 7
UBS Verbier Festival Chamber Orchestra* 40

Index of Works

Bold italic figures refer to Prom numbers (PSM indicates Proms Saturday Matinees: see pages 108–9.
PCM indicates Proms Chamber Music concerts: see pages 110–13)
* First performance at a BBC Henry Wood Promenade Concert

BBC Proms 2006

Director Nicholas Kenyon CBE, Controller, BBC Proms,
Live Events and TV Classical Music
Personal Assistant Yvette Pusey

Artistic Administrator Rosemary Gent
Concerts Administrator Helen Burridge
Concerts Assistants Isabella Kernot, Helen Lloyd
TV Concerts Assistant Tom Nelson

Marketing Manager Kate Finch
Publicist Victoria Bevan
Assistant Publicist Leanne Williams
Marketing Co-ordinator Catherine Chew
Learning and Audience Development Co-ordinator Ellara Wakely
Music Intro Administrator Lydia Casey
Learning Consultant Lincoln Abbotts

Business & Finance Manager David Stott
Management Assistant Tricia Twigg

Editor, Live Music, BBC Radio 3 Edward Blakeman
Editor, TV Classical Music Oliver Macfarlane

BBC Proms 2006 Guide

Editor Mark Pappenheim
Production Manager Sarah Hirons
Design Premm Design Ltd, London
Cover photograph (RAH) Simon Keats

Proms Publications Editor John Bryant
Editorial Manager Edward Bhesania
Publications Designer Tania Conrad
Publications Officer Mary Galloway

Published by BBC Proms Publications, Room 330,
Henry Wood House, 3–6 Langham Place, London W1B 3DF

Distributed by BBC Worldwide, 80 Wood Lane, London W12 0TT

Advertising Cabbell Publishing Ltd, London
Printed by Taylor Bloxham Ltd, Leicester

© BBC 2006   ISBN 0-563-49371-2